THE SECRET
WEDDING

THE SECRET WEDDING

•

Annette Mahon

AVALON BOOKS
NEW YORK

PRINTED IN THE UNITED STATES OF AMERICA
ON ACID-FREE PAPER
BY HADDON CRAFTSMEN, BLOOMSBURG, PENNSYLVANIA

For my daughters, who definitely brought weddings to
the forefront of my mind when two of them decided to marry
in the space of eleven months.
Mrs. Hand and Mrs. Mercey, this is for you.

And not to neglect my bachelorette daughter—
special thanks for setting up my website:
www.annettemahon.com

Chapter One

"**I** owe it all to you!"

Luana Young stood before Emma Correa's teller window in the Malino branch of Statewide Bank. From the window next to Emma's, Kim Asencion peered over. Customers stood patiently in the waiting area, ears alert. Bank business could wait for a few minutes; they were interested in learning more.

"I've been offered a great job," Luana continued, "and it's all because of you."

With a flourish, Luana presented Emma with a bouquet of yellow roses, the edges of their petals tipped with pink.

"So I brought you these as a thank-you."

Emma accepted the vase, taking a deep, appreciative breath.

"They're wonderful. *Mahalo.*"

Luana knew that these particular roses were Emma's favorites. It was what her new husband always ordered for her, and Luana took pride in remembering such particulars about her customers.

"But what's the job?" Emma's dark, curious eyes surveyed her friend.

"You're looking at the new wedding coordinator for the Kukui Wana'ao Resort." Luana grinned. "The manager there called me. Their coordinator quit unexpectedly and he said they needed someone right away, and would I be interested. He remembered me from your wedding. Can you imagine?"

Emma nodded. "You did do a beautiful job with our reception, Luana."

From the milling customers came several voices offering their agreement. All of Malino had attended Emma and Matt's wedding.

Luana shrugged off their praise. "I loved doing it. I wasn't sure about this though. After all, I just did your flowers."

"You did more than that," Emma insisted. "Didn't she, Kim?"

"You did." Kim, Emma's maid of honor, agreed. "You did all the decorations, and coordinated everything with the hotel."

"I guess." Luana's grin faded. "I was so excited that he asked me, I said yes. But now I'm scared. What if I can't do it?"

"Don't be silly. You'll do great," Emma assured her.

"What are you going to do great?" Elderly Mr. Jardine, a regular customer, had just entered the bank. His eyes twinkled as they settled on the bouquet of roses. "Is that husband of yours surprising you again?" he asked Emma.

Both Emma and Luana laughed. One of the beauties of a small town was the interest everyone took in their neighbors' lives. Not too long ago, everyone in town was speculating on the identity of the man who sent Emma beautiful roses "from a secret admirer."

"No. These are from Luana."

Mr. Jardine glanced toward Luana and winked. "I wish I was twenty years younger, Luana. I'd be sending *you* roses."

This brought a laugh from tellers and customers both, and one of the other men slapped Mr. Jardine on the back. Luana's cheeks pinkened.

"So what is it you're going to do?" Mr. Jardine asked again.

Luana grinned. With a little support from her friends, her confidence was back.

"I have a new job."

"A new job, huh? No more selling flowers out of your parents' store?"

"Oh, I'll still be doing that." Luana's parents ran Young's General Store, an all-purpose emporium on Malino's main street. Mr. Young saw to the hardware, the gardening items, and the kitchen supplies. Mrs. Young supervised the small selection of undergarments, the bolts of fabric, and the sewing supplies. Luana provided potted plants, cut flowers, and leis for special occasions. "It was a great job while I was studying, but now that I have my degree, I want something more. I'm going to be wedding coordinator at the Kukui Wana'ao Resort."

"Wow. Congratulations." Mr. Jardine shook Luana's hand. "I wish you success with it. You did a real good job with Emma's wedding."

"Thank you."

Luana's gaze circled the room, taking in her friends and neighbors. "I'm so excited! I can hardly wait to begin."

* * *

Two weeks later, Luana wasn't sure her new job would be the success she had hoped. Not, at least, if she had to work with clients like this one.

She had managed to get through one wedding already— one that had been set up by the former coordinator. It had gone well, thank goodness. The weather had been beautiful, and the bride and groom had expressed their delight with both ceremony and reception.

And she had begun making preparations for the first weddings she was planning on her own. A couple from Denver was flying out in six months, and wanted to be married the weekend of their arrival. They would then honeymoon in one of the private villas at the resort. They were pleasant and easy to work with. Luana had enjoyed speaking to the bride about the arrangements.

And a couple from Seattle was planning a Christmas wedding with her. She'd already had several phone conversations with the bride-to-be and her mother.

But this new client!

Earlier that morning, she had been advised by management to expect his arrival.

"He's a very important client for the hotel, Luana. Show him your best Aloha spirit. And use the utmost discretion, of course."

The general manager's words were a mystery to Luana. Even more so when the client arrived. He had appeared in person—and alone. Then, to make matters worse, he wanted to speak to her about a wedding for someone else entirely! And he wanted everything arranged in a mere four weeks.

"You want me to plan a wedding in four weeks? And it's not even *your* wedding?"

"Yes."

His calm demeanor was frustrating. *He* didn't seem to think it odd that a couple would send a third person to make the arrangements for such a big day. Nor did it seem to occur to him that most couples spent six months to a year planning their wedding day. No wonder the manager had spoken to her about diplomacy and tact.

"But who are the bride and groom? And *where* are they?"

"Who they are isn't important. I'm related to the bride and she asked me to set something up."

To set something up. The words resounded in Luana's head. Did the man have no conception at all of how odd this all sounded?

"Mr., ah . . ." Luana's eyes searched her desk for the man's name. Frustration with the situation, and the stress of trying to remain calm and professional, was making her usually reliable memory faulty. How could she possibly have forgotten his name? *"A very important client for the hotel . . ."* The general manager's words echoed in her ears.

Finally, she saw what she needed, scribbled at the top of her pad of paper. Breathing deeply, she rested her elbows on the edge of her desk and leaned forward. Remembering to give him her best smile, she nonetheless enunciated carefully, her voice earnest.

"Mr. Lawrence. A wedding is a very personal thing. It's a special day for the couple, and especially for the bride— one she'll remember for her entire life. Most women have been planning it since preschool. I don't see how I can arrange a wedding if I can't speak to the couple. Or at least to the bride."

Mr. Lawrence was unfazed. He smiled. "Please, call me Jake."

Luana stared. Mr. Lawrence—Jake—had a beautiful smile. Apologetic even. Dimples appeared. The corners of his eyes crinkled, and his head tilted to a most attractive angle. His hair was short, a light brown with "natural" highlights that must have come from a bottle; his face was too pale for the sun to account for it. It looked like he'd been running his fingers through it, but Luana knew that disheveled look was the latest hot new fashion. Her stylish oldest brother had tried it; on him it merely looked messy. On Jake Lawrence, it achieved its aim, a combination of boyishness and just-out-of-bed sexiness.

Luana gazed into his pale eyes, mesmerized by their unusual (for Hawaii, anyway) azure color and the sparkling good humor she saw there.

As he saw her intent observation of him, he increased the wattage of the smile. The dimples deepened. Luana swallowed. He must have been the most attractive man she'd ever met. Certainly the most elegant, if you could use that word to describe a man. His modish hairstyle, the designer polo shirt, the chic cut of his slacks—all indicated a man who knew his way in the world. Sangfroid. That's what he had.

Then she came to her senses. Yes, he was a good-looking man, but he was a vacationing man, a client, with a home on the mainland. A man who obviously lived in an environment miles away from her own, both literally and figuratively. She'd do well to remember that in her dealings with him, and to keep their relationship on a professional level.

Besides, she told herself, *he's using his good looks to win you over. Look at that smile!* Did he practice in front of a mirror? How else could he get it just right, just hinting at those dimples in his cheeks? How else achieve that boy-ish look by tilting his head just so?

Luana felt better after noting his adept manner. She could now meet those incredible eyes without drowning in them. She fixed an earnest expression on her face to await his reply. It wasn't what she'd hoped to hear.

"I have the full confidence of the bride. I assure you she will be delighted with all that we do."

Jake smiled again. But Luana was having none of his Mr. Charming routine. She frowned at him. However, she did pull a sheet of paper forward. After all, he was a guest at the resort—apparently a very important guest—and it was her job to help him with his wedding. Or rather, the wedding he wanted to "set up."

"It's a strange way to arrange a wedding, Mr. Lawrence. Jake," she amended as she noticed him about to interrupt. "But of course I can do it." She resisted the urge to add "if you insist." Instead she looked up at him hopefully, just in case there had been a change of mind in the last few minutes. Of course there had not. He returned her gaze with a steady, expectant regard.

Luana sighed. "I would still feel better if I could consult with the bride."

"Maybe I could arrange for you to speak to her by phone."

Luana brightened. He didn't sound confident, but it was a start. Perhaps working with him wouldn't be too difficult after all.

"That would be good." It was a small concession, but boded well. If she could actually talk to the bride, she wouldn't feel quite so strange about the whole thing.

She picked up her pen and held it poised over her form. "What is the bride's name?"

It was Jake's turn to frown. "I told you it's not necessary for you to have that information. I'll be handling all the arrangements, and signing all the checks."

"You want me to plan a wedding and reception for a couple, but you don't want to give me their names?"

"That's right."

Luana thought his smile might be turning brittle. Hers certainly was.

"If you need a name for your form, you can call them Mr. and Mrs. Smith."

"Very original." Luana wasn't sure she was hiding her frustration, although she was trying. And despite the fact that she thought the muttered words were indecipherable, he apparently heard them clearly enough.

"The groom's last name does happen to be Smith," Jake told her.

Luana stared at him for a moment. He did appear to be telling the truth. "Okay." She tapped the paper on her desk with the wrong end of her pen. "However, it's usual to designate two names when referring to a wedding. The Brown-Talbot wedding, for example. The bride's name is stated first."

Jake sighed. How had he gotten into this situation?

He knew how, of course, but *why* had he allowed his little sister to talk him into this? "Set up a wedding for me, Jake," she'd said. "But don't let anybody know. We *have* to keep it a secret, and you know how difficult that will be. But I know you can do it."

He loved his baby half-sister, and he'd done a lot to help her career. He understood her concerns, knew they were real. But still . . .

Here he was, at a posh, private resort in Hawaii, sitting before a beautiful woman who thought he was a total flake.

His famous charm wasn't working on her, that was obvious. And the fact that it wasn't bothered him more than he cared to admit. He was losing his touch, and he wasn't even thirty-one years old.

Luana Young, the resort's wedding coordinator, had a nice face. Not classically beautiful, but open and friendly, not to mention exotically pretty. He was intrigued by her eyes. They were so dark they should have been mysterious. But instead they were friendly and welcoming. Until he began to evade her questions. Then they became eerily similar to the eyes of Mrs. Frankhurst, his third-grade teacher and his favorite teacher ever. She'd had a way of looking at you, if you did poorly on a test, or didn't turn in an assignment. It was a look that said she could hardly believe it; *how* could you disappoint her this way? Luana Young had that same ability, to look . . . vulnerable, perhaps. It was a powerful attribute, especially for a teacher, and made every last student feel guilty. It was no different now with Luana. He wanted to tell her everything. Of course, he could not. The open friendliness he had first observed in Luana made him feel sure he could trust her with the real story. Why should she care who was being married, after all? But events from Callie's past flooded his mind along with horror stories he'd heard about the activities surrounding celebrity weddings. But most important, he'd promised Callie.

He tried his smile once again, but she merely stared at him. "Can we call it the Smith-Lawrence wedding?"

"Shouldn't it be the Lawrence-Smith wedding?" Her brows reached toward her hairline. "If *she's* a relative of yours?"

"It would be better if we reversed the names."

He thought he heard her sigh. But she didn't argue.

"If we must," she muttered.

Once again, he heard her clearly although he thought she hoped he didn't. It made him smile.

"And the exact wedding date?" Her voice was back at a normal volume.

"Four weeks from today."

"A Wednesday?"

Luana raised an eyebrow but didn't comment. At his nod, she consulted her computer. Pulling up the hotel events calendar, he assumed. She frowned at the screen for a long time.

"How many people will be attending?"

"It will be an intimate affair, about a hundred and fifty people. No more than two hundred."

Luana's eyebrows drew up almost to her hairline. Jake suddenly realized that to the general population, an intimate affair would probably indicate a group of ten to twenty. Darn, he'd been associating with Callie and her crowd for far too long. If he was going to keep this whole thing a secret for Callie, he was going to have to adjust his thinking.

"Two hundred total," Luana repeated. Her eyes went back to the screen. "I'm sure we can manage it. Four weeks is incredibly short notice, though, especially for a wedding. Functions here are usually arranged months or even years in advance."

"But you could manage it?"

"I think so. We have several options available. It will depend on exactly what kind of wedding you have in mind."

Luana glanced back toward him. She did have the most incredible eyes. Once again, he felt guilty for causing her so many problems. He'd like to get to know her, but right now he knew he didn't stand a chance. While it might not be contempt spilling from her eyes, he felt fairly certain it was dislike.

"Are you sure the couple wouldn't want to wait a little longer? Even a few months would make all the difference in planning a truly lovely ceremony."

Jake had to grin. "Do you mean you won't be able to plan a 'truly lovely ceremony' for four weeks from today?"

He'd finally managed to ruffle her feathers. She had such expressive eyes!

Luana scrambled to reassure him. But Jake felt sure what she really wanted to do was slap him. He found the thought entertaining. Yes, she would be a fun date; not at all in his usual line.

"I'm sure we'll be able to arrange a wedding to remember. It's just that the more time we have, the easier it is to be sure everything will be just as you want it."

Jake watched her for a moment. He'd spoken to the resort manager before he'd approached Luana. He needed reassurances that the ceremony and reception could be held in the strictest privacy. He felt sure the manager would have said something to his wedding coordinator. Apparently, he hadn't said much. Which was just what Jake had requested. It gave him confidence about the discretion of the resort and its personnel.

Luana was peering up at him with an expectant expression. She probably hoped that her little speech would change his mind. No use letting her think that she could do that.

"I don't think the bride is willing to wait."

"Perhaps if you explained to her—about the timing and how really rushed this would be?"

Jake shook his head. "I could talk to her, but I doubt if

it will make any difference." He glanced at his watch. "The time difference makes it complicated to get in touch with her. That's why I don't know if I can arrange a phone conversation."

He let his voice trail off. What was he doing? He was the client here, and it was up to her to do as he requested. He was letting her soulful eyes get to him. It appeared she wasn't averse to using her looks to get her way. He wondered if she practiced that appealing look in the mirror, tilting her head slightly upward and widening her eyes. It made her look so helpless and in need of protection. The sweet expression suddenly looked manipulative; maybe he didn't want to get to know her after all.

Straightening his shoulders, Jake cleared his throat. "I will speak to her, but I doubt I'll be able to change her mind. She's always had a mind of her own," he added with a wry downturn of his mouth. "Meanwhile, could you begin preparations? Since you've mentioned the short time available?"

"Of course." Luana frowned. "However, I can't do much without having a great deal more information. I'll need specific choices concerning food, music, and flowers. Will the groom and groomsmen be bringing their clothes or would I have to arrange for tuxes?"

When he didn't answer immediately, she continued.

"Then there are the photographer, videographer, the cake. I'll need the bride's theme and her preferences for the color scheme. I need to know if the ceremony itself will be here at the resort or at a church. And do I need to make the arrangements for the church or the minister or the judge?"

Luana noticed that Jake was beginning to look panicky. Her lips parted in a satisfied smile. Good. He had no idea what he expected her to do, and in such a short time. This was supposed to be a part-time job for her, but it would take a week of twelve-hour days to get all the arrangements made in the short time that he demanded. And she still had her small flower business in Malino to attend to.

Luana smiled sweetly as his eyes shifted and his skin paled. She almost felt sorry for him. Men had no idea about weddings! Luana felt sure the bride would be on the phone with her before morning.

Chapter Two

Luana received several phone calls pertaining to planned weddings on Wednesday afternoon, but none came from a bride related to Jake Lawrence. Jake himself appeared at her desk promptly at nine o'clock on Thursday morning. He flashed his charming smile, the one that made the corners of his eyes crinkle and his dimples flash. The one that made him look good enough to eat.

The one she was sure he must practice in front of the mirror, she reminded herself. No one could be that gorgeous without working at it.

Seated, with her notes before her, Luana frowned. Why did she keep thinking of him in terms of "charming"? Was it some remnant of fairy tales read to her when she was a child? She had to get herself in order. It wouldn't do to keep thinking like some delirious child searching for a Prince Charming. This was a business relationship, and should be contained on that level. She *would not* notice his smile. Or his dimples. Or the way his eyes flashed when he laughed.

Finishing her lecture to herself, Luana stood and offered her hand across the desk. She smiled, as well. A nice, professional smile, she felt. Not too wide, but friendly. Welcoming.

"Good morning, Mr. Lawrence."

Jake took her hand, increasing the wattage of his smile. "Now, Luana, I thought we had gotten beyond 'Mr.' yesterday. It's Jake, remember?"

"Yes, of course." She smiled again. "Jake."

Luana's smile faltered as Jake continued to hold her hand in his. Shaking his hand had been a big mistake. But how could she possibly have known? His hand was hard and masculine, and very warm. She could feel the heat of it warming her hand, cool from the air-conditioning in her office. The warmth traveled up her arm, reaching beyond her proffered limb to her neck and her cheeks.

Luana pulled her eyes from his, looking pointedly at their still-joined hands. She didn't want to be rude and pull her hand abruptly from his, but the heat had now reached beyond her neck and face and was tripping down her spine. It was all she could do to hold her posture; she wanted to wriggle from the strange sensation.

No, he was the one being boorish, she reminded herself. Perhaps men acted this way in the big cities on the mainland, but here it was not considered the thing to do more than offer a brief handshake. Theirs was a business relationship after all.

If Jake thought it odd that he still held her hand, he didn't show it by look or action. In fact he reached up with his other hand, cradling her right hand gently, treating it like some precious object that he had been specially chosen to guard.

Luana could feel the heat in her cheeks increase. Wondering if her face was bright red, she chanced an upward glance. His eyes caught hers once again, gazing reverently, almost questioningly, into hers. It wouldn't have surprised her if he'd raised her hand to his lips and bestowed a gallant kiss thereto.

Thereto? Oh, boy, she was letting this Prince Charming stuff really mess with her head.

With a definitive movement, she retrieved her hand, seated herself behind her desk, and gestured for him to sit as well. If he thought her rude, so be it. The man was insufferable; she was sure he'd done that on purpose, trying to flatter her with his attention so that she would move along with the plans for his strange wedding without asking too many questions.

She ignored the captivating smile hovering on his lips. A smile that indicated he knew how she felt about his touch. Her cheeks pink with simmering anger, she cleared her throat and got right to the point.

"Did you have a chance to talk to the bride last night? The future Mrs., ah, Smith?"

He grinned. "That really is his name, you know."

His voice was low. Seductive almost. It seemed to move against her skin like sandpaper on smooth wood—irritating, but ultimately soothing.

Luana blinked across her desk at him, working to banish her strange daydreams and newly lyrical mental images. She seized at the reality of replying to his statement and re-asking her question.

"Of course." She might not believe the couple would really be Mr. and Mrs. Smith, but she could certainly agree with him. "Did you speak to the future Mrs. Smith about the wedding?"

"Yes, I did."

Jake saw delight flood Luana's open face as her smile widened. No longer merely polite, this smile made her eyes sparkle and her lips eminently kissable. He'd resisted an irrational impulse earlier to kiss her hand—like some kind of knight errant. He was glad there was a desk between them now. This time the desire was to kiss her lips, and this was more than an impulse. Without the impediment of the large piece of furniture, Jake was afraid he would have succumbed. Luana had wide, full lips. He'd like nothing better than to touch her lower lip, to feel the firm, soft texture of it, to taste its sweetness. He'd bet his plane ticket home there was no collagen there providing that pleasing plumpness.

Jake raked his eyes back up to focus on her full face, thrusting thoughts of her lips aside. He finally seated himself in the chair she'd indicated earlier, determined to stick to business. Watching her expressive face, he thought it just as well she had not heard his actual conversation with Callie.

Jake winced inwardly at the memory of his call to his half-sister. He'd caught her in the limo, in Milwaukee, on her way to do the sound check. She had not been in the best of moods, whining at his greeting.

"Callie, dearest sister. I need some help with the wedding details."

"Ja-ake. I'm busy."

He apologized for calling. Touring was a grind, he knew that. She was traveling every few days, up till all hours working. And the whole time, she was virtually a prisoner in her hotel room unless she wanted to chance going out and being recognized. In that case, she would be swamped by fans, autograph-seekers, and paparazzi.

But he had to tell her about the hundreds of details necessary to planning a wedding, details normally handled by the bride. He didn't blame her for not realizing there was so much involved. He hadn't known either.

Callie, however, was far from cooperative. She was in one of her moods, definitely being the spoiled darling of pop.

"Honestly, Jake. I just want to get married. How hard could it be? People do it all the time."

"Callie, you have no idea." He sighed as he recalled the dozens of minute details Luana had raised. "There are lots of things I don't even begin to know about. Are you sure you don't want to talk to the hotel's planner? I've been told that women have very definite ideas about these things."

This time it was Callie who sighed. Jake heard it clearly over the phone line. Yesterday had been a traveling day. Maybe she hadn't gotten enough sleep. That would affect her mood.

"I got my dress. I got a designer in London to fax me some designs and I picked one. She's sending someone out to measure me so they can be sure it fits right. Tommy is going to wear a white suit."

"That's great." Jake was encouraged. So she had done more than just *think* about getting married.

But any hopes he'd had that she had done any planning beyond arranging for a gown evaporated at her next words.

"Jake, the limo's slowing—I gotta go. I just want to have a nice wedding, okay?" Her voice took on a wheedling tone. "I know you can do it. You're so good at that detail stuff."

That was it. She'd disconnected. Just before she did, he

could hear noise—the shouting of a crowd of crazed fans. They would be waiting at the venue, hoping to catch a glimpse of the performers. Callie was working now. If he called back, the phone would be off. He'd have to handle the decision-making on his own.

Any urge to share the truth with Luana died when he saw the hopeful gleam in her eyes. He couldn't burst her balloon by telling her how casually Callie was handling her wedding. Luana took weddings seriously, that was obvious from her job. She probably knew, in great detail, everything she wanted for her own wedding. She wouldn't understand a young woman who didn't seem to care about such things.

Callie had always lived in a world of her own. It was part of her creative spirit, part of what made her such a great performer. But it was impractical. Especially now. And of course, she was very young. Too young to get married, he thought. But she hadn't listened to him or to their father when they'd suggested she wait. And she was old enough legally not to need permission from anyone.

Callie had always been one for immediate gratification. Actually, it was amazing that she had given him four weeks. He wouldn't have been surprised if she had eloped to Vegas, standing up with Tommy before an Elvis impersonator. He was almost sorry she hadn't done it that way. It would have saved them all a lot of trouble. Though perhaps the media circus that would have followed an elopement would have been more of a problem than this secrecy.

He looked again into Luana's open, honest face. She moved in a world completely different from Callie's. She wouldn't understand, would be shocked at Callie's indifferent attitude. So he decided to let her believe he had learned all Callie's choices when he called. He was just going to have to make the decisions himself. It was, after all, what Callie wanted. He was a businessman who made important decisions every day. How hard could it be?

Luana seemed to be expecting him to say something. Had she asked a question that he hadn't heard while ruminating over yesterday's phone conversation? He raised a brow at her, asking a silent question. She seemed to hear it.

"So, what did she say?"

"Well . . ." Jake wasn't sure how much he should admit. "She has her wedding dress."

Encouraged by the smile Luana bestowed on him, he went on. "And she said the groom will be wearing a white suit."

"Great."

Luana flashed a smile that sent shivers up his spine. He couldn't understand this effect she had on him. She was an attractive woman, though her looks were a world removed from the models and starlets he usually dated. As one of the best-known entertainment lawyers in California, Jake never lacked a beautiful woman to grace his arm.

"Is her gown a long, formal dress, or a more casual style?"

Jake's mind was blank. Callie hadn't said. Would she even know? Most women knew things like that, but Callie wasn't most women.

"She said it was from a designer in London."

Luana stared at Jake. She appeared to be waiting for him to say more. When he didn't, she spoke.

"There are several well-known designers in London who specialize in wedding gowns. Did she give you the designer's name?"

Jake frowned and Luana knew that he had no idea who it was. If only they had met in other circumstances. He was such a handsome man, she would have enjoyed getting to know him—if she hadn't been trying to plan a wedding for him and meeting obstacles at every turn.

"The designer faxed her a sketch of the dress. I'll see if she could fax me a copy."

"That would be good."

Luana made a note and looked up again. "So what did she say about colors and theme? And did she mention what kind of flowers she likes?"

Jake released a long breath. She also noted a swallow deep enough that she could see it move down his throat. Luana sagged in her chair. He didn't know. It was obvious from his body language that he couldn't answer any of her questions. How did he ever expect this to work?

"Callie loves flowers of all kinds. Especially fragrant flowers."

Luana nodded, but she recognized evasion. "And the colors?"

Once again she noted the deep swallow. He didn't give too much away, but she had a feeling his mind was whirling, trying to come up with answers for her. It just wasn't going to work.

"Is her dress all she talked about?" She tried to keep the incredulity from her voice, but it was a losing battle. Jake had to know how peculiar she thought this whole situation.

"Look. I realize the circumstances here are difficult. But eventually, you'll realize why it's necessary."

He ran his hand through his hair, front to back. It fell back into place, looking basically as it had before. Tousled. Still, Luana couldn't resist a small smile. The gesture made him more accessible somehow, friendly and boyish. The bleached highlights reminded her of the young surfer boys from the islands. If he was darker-skinned, and didn't have those incredible pale eyes . . .

Luana pulled herself back to the business at hand.

"Didn't she even mention the color of her attendants' gowns?"

Jake didn't reply, just looked uncomfortable for a moment. Then he seemed to recover his poise, and sat up straight. He offered his smile, the one that oozed charm.

"Look, how about meeting for lunch? I feel bad about this whole thing, but it's not really up to me to decide how much to tell you. In this situation, I'm basically an employee, and I have to listen to my employer."

Luana was confused, and didn't mind showing it. "I thought the bride was a relative of yours?"

"Yes." Once again the charming smile. "As I said, it's complicated."

Jake stood. "I'll see if I can get through to her now. She was in a rush when I called last night. The time differences, you know. And she's a very busy person, with a lot of professional commitments. Hopefully, I'll have some answers for you at lunch. My treat, of course," he added.

Suddenly he was all efficiency, looking pointedly at the papers spread out on her desk.

"Do you have everything you want covered listed on those papers? If you give me copies, I'll know what I'm supposed to ask her."

Suddenly, Luana felt sorry for him. The bride had put him in an awkward position, though he had allowed it. So he wasn't without blame. But it was obvious to her that he'd had no idea what he was getting into. She didn't have to check his left hand to know he wasn't married. The man had bachelor written all over him.

She reached into one of the desk drawers, pulling out a thin booklet.

"Look, why don't you check this over. It's a wedding planner. They make them for brides. It lists everything that has to be done for a wedding, with the time indicated." She couldn't resist opening it up and showing him the first page. "You see, here it says Twelve Months Before, Six Months Before, et cetera."

Jake accepted the booklet graciously, ignoring the pointed reference to timing. "Thank you. I'm sure this will be a big help."

He folded the booklet in half and tucked it into his back pocket.

"I'll make a reservation for us in the Terrace Restaurant. Why don't you meet me there at noon?"

Although he'd phrased it as a question, Jake turned and fled her office without waiting for an answer.

Luana watched him leave. Darn, but he was great to look at! His polo-style shirt showed off muscular arms. His jeans conformed to his strong legs. Whatever he did for a living, he obviously took time out for exercise. Good-looking, coming or going!

Luana continued to stare at the empty door, startled at herself. Heat flooded her face. She'd never had thoughts like this about a man before in her life. She'd grown up in a small town, led a sheltered existence. Her family had high moral standards that she upheld. While many of the town's young people left every year, fleeing to cities on the mainland, Luana *liked* small-town living. She'd spent time in Honolulu and knew the impersonal city lifestyle was not for her. Jake Lawrence was definitely having a deleterious effect on her.

Luana sighed. If only he would take the future Mrs.

Smith's wedding and find somewhere else to hold it! Somehow she thought the possibility remote, but she couldn't help wishing. Perhaps she'd drop a penny in the fountain in the main courtyard on her way out. It couldn't hurt.

Chapter Three

J ake sat at a table for two in the Terrace, wondering if Luana would appear. He stirred his iced tea with the narrow stick of sugar cane, staring at the mini-whirlpool he created as the ice cubes moved in rapid circles in the limited space. He'd been preemptory, he realized, telling her to come instead of asking her to meet him. While that type of commanding attitude appealed to some women, he was sure Luana would not appreciate it. And it was not in his usual style. He usually had enough regard for a woman to solicit her opinion.

Jake poked at the ice with the sugar cane. It was too late for regrets. He'd just have to be more careful in the future if he wanted to remain on Luana's good side. And since he found her strangely appealing, he wanted to be friends— for at least as long as it took to explore these unusual and interesting feelings.

In the two hours since he'd rushed out of Luana's office,

he'd managed to reach Callie's best friend, Stacey Albright, and settle most of the pressing questions about the wedding. Not one to take to other girls, Callie had nonetheless forged a close relationship with Stacey that had lasted many years. Originally her dance instructor and now her choreographer, less than ten years in age separated them, even though Stacey had been giving her dance lessons since Callie was a child. As Callie grew older, the dance lessons had evolved into dance routines to incorporate into her act.

Through Stacey, Jake had obtained a description of Callie's gown for Luana and discovered that the attendants would be wearing shorter, plainer versions of the wedding gown in gold.

"The designer said that's the real traditional thing to do," Stacey had told him, "having the attendants dress in a style similar to the bride's." Then she'd giggled. "Can you imagine—Callie actually doing the traditional thing?"

He'd laughed too. It was inconsistent all right, but showed that Callie was maturing. He hoped.

As they spoke, Jake checked over the booklet Luana had given him, conferring with Stacey on anything he didn't feel confident deciding on his own.

Now he looked up as the hostess approached his table, hoping it would be Luana arriving for their meeting. But the attractive middle-aged woman was leading an elderly couple across the terrace, finally seating them at the edge of the lanai where they had a beautiful view of the ocean.

Long and narrow, the restaurant boasted a wall of glass offering spectacular ocean views. Tables were grouped on both sides of the glass wall, which was interrupted by several wide, open doors. These allowed entry to the clean sea breeze. But Jake had asked to be seated outside. Why not enjoy the full effect of the beautiful climate?

As he waited, Jake entertained himself watching the antics of the island birds. Mostly sparrows and finches, but including a few small black-and-white birds with red heads that he could not identify, they clustered around the outdoor tables, edging closer and closer to the diners. An abandoned plate was fair game, soon having its remnants sought after by several competing fellows. Although printed notes on each table asked diners not to feed the birds, Jake noticed many of the tourists ignored the warning and threw bread crumbs to the little beggars.

Then he saw her, just stepping into the space between the open doors. Standing there like a bird ready to flutter off at the merest suggestion of movement, Luana paused for a moment, one foot poised on the threshold, looking around at the crowded outdoor tables.

Jake straightened, releasing the sugar cane, which continued to spin for a few seconds longer. Where had that poetic image come from? He could be a romantic guy, it was true, but such thoughts were usually deliberate on his part, offered to dates to gain favor. But today's reflection on Luana's similarity to a bird had come on its own, out of nowhere.

Shaking off the troubling thought, Jake rose. He'd best forget such extraneous musings and greet his guest. He'd probably been watching the birds for too long—that was where that image had originated, of course.

Luana was entering the terrace proper now, her blue-and-purple figured muumuu swaying seductively around her as she walked. All the women employed in the hotel offices wore this same blue-and-purple garment, yet only Luana made it seem seductive. There was something about the way the garment moved as she did, hinting at the active body beneath. The Victorians might have had the right idea, covering the female figure to make it more interesting and enticing—if that had been their goal.

Jake stepped forward, helping Luana with her chair. First, he had to tear his eyes away from her hips and their gentle movement. He wouldn't want her to think he was a lecher. His mama taught him how to treat a woman and it was past time he showed Luana his excellent manners.

"I'm glad you could join me."

He pushed her chair in and returned to his own place, flashing his finest smile. "I was on the elevator when I realized that I didn't give you a chance to agree, just presumed on your time. I hope you'll forgive me."

Luana nodded graciously. Everything she did was graceful. He'd been around performers for years, yet Luana had something special. He wondered if she was a dancer. He knew the Islands were famous for their graceful dancers and it was a role he could easily imagine Luana filling.

Thinking how little he knew of her, and even of the Islands, gave him an idea.

"Luana, I think we've gotten off to bad start. Can we start over?" He met her confused gaze with his most sincere look. It was easy. He wasn't acting; he really did want to start over with her.

"Let's pretend that we've just met, that we're going to get to know each other over lunch, and then we're going to so some business together. What do you say?"

Luana looked into Jake's clear blue eyes. He was no longer flashing that dimpled smile, the practiced one that made her so suspicious. And his eyes were sincere. She could trust a man with eyes like those, so deep and soulful.

So her original, persistent image of him smiling in front of a mirror faded and she returned his smile.

"You want to put off discussing the wedding until after lunch?"

Jake nodded, his lips tipping up slightly to the left in a tentative smile.

Luana took another moment to examine his face, then nodded her own agreement. After all, hadn't she been told to treat him well? It was her responsibility as a dedicated employee of the Kukui Wana'ao to accede to his wishes.

"It's a deal." She offered her hand across the narrow table. "It's a pleasure to meet you, Mr. Lawrence." She had to suppress an urge to giggle in a most unladylike way at the pretense.

"It's Jake. Please." But his voice was easy, not insistent.

"And of course you must call me Luana."

Their waitress appeared, pencil poised above her order book, her smile wide and gracious.

"Aloha. Are you ready to order?"

Luana felt self-conscious eating in the resort restaurant as Jake's guest. She'd brought clients here herself since taking the job, but then they were her guests, which was quite a different thing. And they came at off hours, to sample the food so that the bridal couples could make informed choices, not during the busy lunch period. Jake, however, was an expert at social chatter, and by the time their salads appeared, he had Luana at her ease.

They spoke of general things over the meal—his impression of the Islands, then movies, and going on to music. As she expected, Jake claimed to love the Islands' beauty and laid-back atmosphere. It was the same thing all the guests said. He did admit, however, that the relaxed pace of daily life was taking some getting used to. It was no more than she had expected; Jake was obviously someone used to big city life.

It was when they moved into what Luana considered the more "social" topics that she really began to enjoy herself. It had been a long time since she'd found someone with so many similar interests. Jake was far more knowledgeable than Luana about movies, but she enjoyed them and went often. She was also quite willing to debate the merits of *Star Wars* versus *Star Trek,* or whether sequels ever lived up to the original film.

In music, both had eclectic tastes. Jake seemed to know all the current bands and singers, both rock and country, while Luana was familiar with only a handful.

"I guess taste in music is like taste in art. I know what I like." She laughed. "There are so many groups and soloists these days, I can't keep up with them all. So I don't even try. But I love Hawaiian music, and I do try to keep up with the new groups here."

"Now there's an area I don't know much about," Jake admitted. "But I'd like to learn. Maybe I can catch some acts while I'm here working on the wedding."

"A good idea." Luana smiled encouragement. "I can recommend some good performers. Starting with the group who entertains here on the Terrace during dinner."

"Thanks for the recommendation. I'll be sure to catch them."

Jake pushed aside his plate, finished with his meal. "Did you ever do any performing? Dancing, perhaps?"

Luana raised her eyebrows. "How did you know?" After her initial surprised reaction, Luana lowered her eyes, embarrassed by his attention to what she considered a very personal side of her life. She took the narrow orange slice that garnished her plate, twisting it with her fingers as she spoke. "I dance. Well, I danced, I guess I should say. I haven't been doing much dancing recently. But I performed all through high school and college."

"Why did you give it up?"

"Dancing hula is more than just the performance. It's a whole lifestyle." Luana bit into the slice of orange and placed the mangled strip of peel on her plate. "Once I finished my schooling, I knew I had to get on with a career. And I decided it wouldn't be dancing; I want a career in something more reliable than the entertainment business."

Jake nodded seriously enough, but he seemed to be trying to suppress a smile, making Luana pause. But he didn't comment on her conception of the entertainment world, so she continued.

"It's a difficult business at the best of times, and dependent on the tourist industry which is also unreliable. And then age makes a huge difference. So once I graduated, I started working harder at my florist business. I'd been selling plants and flowers through my parents' store all through high school and college, and I've been trying to expand it a little. Then I was offered the job here, so you might say I've gotten into the wedding business now." She smiled at him. "While the flowers and the weddings tie together, there just isn't time to devote to dancing. I hope I'll be able to get back to it someday. Maybe later, someday when I have a family of my own."

She had barely finished speaking when their waitress appeared with the dessert menu. Luana quickly declined anything more, claiming to be filled. Jake also passed on dessert, but requested coffee.

Once their waitress left, Jake turned to Luana.

"I guess that's the end of our business-free truce." He spread his hands before his chest. "I'm all yours. Start with your questions."

Luana pulled over the folder she'd brought with her, surprised at how reluctant she was to turn their meeting from social to business. It was a startling revelation, but she had been having a wonderful time. And with this man she had taken into such immediate dislike at their first meeting yesterday. It just went to show that one shouldn't rely on first impressions.

Luana arranged her face into what she felt was a proper business expression and opened the folder to the first sheet of paper, covered with scribbling from their first meeting. She brought out a clean notepad from beneath the folder and pulled a pen from her purse.

"Okay. I'm ready."

She looked up, eyes wide and expectant.

Jake didn't say anything, just enjoyed watching her. He wished he could determine what he found so intriguing about this young woman. She wasn't pretty in a cover model sense, though she was very attractive. Her face was full, saved from roundness by a high forehead and a well-defined chin. Her nose was a little too large, her lips full. But her eyes! Large and almost black, they tipped up at the outer corners to give her the exotic look of a cat woman. These wonderful eyes were framed with thick dark lashes that curled upward, framing her eyes with dark lines reminiscent of the early Egyptians' kohl.

"Uh, Jake?"

He was still looking into her eyes, enchanted by the range of emotions he could read there.

He blinked. "Yes?"

"I said I'm ready. Do you just want to tell me what you've learned, or shall I ask questions?"

Jake offered a wry smile. "You'd better ask. I'm sure

I'll forget half the important things I've discovered if I just talk."

He couldn't help but notice the approval that danced in her eyes. She probably thought he'd spent the time between their meetings speaking to the bride, getting her to make all the important decisions. He wouldn't disillusion her.

He knew his decision was the correct one when she gave him a gracious smile, then began going down her list. This time, he was able to fill in her blanks with a minimum of hesitation.

"I still wish you could talk the bride into giving us a little more time." Luana's brows drew together, and a faint line appeared across her forehead. Her lips drew slightly downward in concern. "You know, most people take a year to plan their weddings."

"I gathered that from your planning leaflet." Jake let his voice reflect his wry mood. He felt sure part of her strategy in giving him the booklet was to let him see the time frame divisions in it. "But with Callie . . ." Jake shrugged. "It's her age. She's young and it's all instant gratification these days. If she decides she wants to be married, then she wants to be married. Consider yourself lucky to have four weeks."

"Why doesn't she just elope?"

Jake looked into her face, but she was just curious.

He hesitated. "There are . . . reasons."

"Sorry. I guess I shouldn't have asked."

Luana smiled an apology, but he could see she had retreated into herself. The friendly companion of lunch, the companion whose company he'd so enjoyed, was completely gone now. The businesswoman was back in control.

Not for the first time, Jake regretted the need for secrecy. He'd like to see Luana's eyes if she heard whose wedding she was arranging. He felt sure she would be excited, like a child with a secret. But unlike the child who would blurt out her secret at the first opportunity, Jake knew Luana would keep it safe.

"I know you said there were good reasons for trying to plan this whole thing without meeting the couple."

Her voice and her facial expression clearly told him that *she* couldn't imagine what these reasons might be. Once again he was tempted to tell her. But he'd promised, and, old-fashioned as it seemed, he was a man of his word.

The realization that he couldn't be entirely truthful with her soured the good time he'd had so far. He pushed aside his empty coffee cup.

"Is that it?"

He almost winced at the abruptness of his tone, but Luana merely set her lips and glanced over her notes.

"There are still a few things that are undecided. Whether or not to get a unity candle. The centerpieces. The music is the biggest thing. There's time to decide on that unless you want live musicians. We can use CDs with no problem, and those can be chosen at the last minute."

"I hadn't thought about whether we'd have live music at both the ceremony and the reception, or at just one or the other."

He stopped to consider it. He had assumed there would be live musicians. But perhaps it would be better without. It not only gave him more time, it opened a wide range of tunes in all types of styles.

"Actually, CDs will probably be better."

Jake felt himself warmed by Luana's smiling approval.

"It does make a much broader range of music available," she said. One side of Luana's mouth tipped up as she gazed at him. "Are you sure you don't want the traditional wedding march?"

Jake grinned. "I can say with assurance that the bride would storm out of the room rather than walk down the aisle to that quaint tune."

"Quaint." Luana raised a brow. She herself loved the traditional wedding trappings, including the music. Like most brides, she couldn't imagine walking down the aisle to anything else.

But Jake was nodding. "Mind you, I have no problems with Wagner, or Mendelssohn either, but for this wedding we'll need something else."

Well, he might not agree with her personal choice, but at least the man was knowledgeable. Not everyone knew that Wagner had composed the well-known "Here Comes the Bride" music.

"The 'Hawaiian Wedding Song' perhaps?" Luana suggested.

Jake seemed to consider it. This was one piece of Hawaiian music he was familiar with. "I do know the piece. . . ."

Luana had to laugh. "Not the Elvis version, I hope."

He laughed too, acknowledging that he was aware of that rendition.

But he finally shook his head. "The 'Hawaiian Wedding Song' is a bit solemn for Callie. We'll need something modern. I'll think about it and let you know."

As Jake helped her rise from the table, Luana smiled at him. It was a pleasant smile, that shone from her eyes as well as her lips.

"I like the bride's colors. Gold and white will be very elegant. And since you've left the flowers up to me, I think I'll use all white."

Her voice was eager as she described the possibilities.

"There are endless varieties of white flowers to choose

from here in the Islands, and some of them are fabulous. I'll bring some brochures over with different styles of bouquets for you to check out. I realize that it's hard for someone to visualize what I'm talking about if I use florist terminology. And knowing what style you feel the bride would prefer will help me chose the type of flowers to use."

"Great. Shall I see you tomorrow then?"

Luana nodded, and Jake watched her go, struck all over again by the graceful movement of her body in its loose garment as she strode away from him.

Feeling fidgety now that the decisions had been made, Jake felt a stroll along the beach might be just what he needed. The resort didn't boast acres of white sand, but a paved path had been provided between the natural, rocky shoreline, and the man-made lagoon closer in. It made for a nice stroll, where he could appreciate the briny sea air, even enjoy the salty mist on his skin, yet avoid getting sand in his shoes.

He whistled softly under his breath as he walked. Yes, this wedding thing wasn't so hard after all. He was a businessman, had been making major decisions for years; things that were more important than the color scheme of Callie's wedding, or whether or not they should have a unity candle.

Smiling in satisfaction at himself, Jake stepped aside to avoid the splash from an incoming wave. A shapely woman in a bikini walking toward him winked, but Jake didn't notice. He was still seeing dark cat eyes smiling up at him and shapely hips covered by blue and purple swaying to and fro.

Chapter Four

Luana stood at a table in the back of Young's General Store, the headquarters of Luana's Tropical Flowers, her fledgling business enterprise. While she'd been supplying her parents' store with potted plants and cut flowers since her high-school days, it had only been a year since she'd gotten her degree and determined to make more of her little business. She had several steady customers, including three local businesses that paid her a monthly fee to supply their offices with fresh floral arrangements.

Luana was busy creating one of these bouquets, while she talked to her friend Mele who waited tables at the restaurant just up the street from the General Store. Mele often stopped by for a visit during the restaurant's off hours.

"So you're having second thoughts about the new job?"

"It isn't that." Luana was having a hard time explaining to Mele her frustration over her new client. "It's just this one man. He wants me to arrange a wedding in four weeks.

37

Four weeks! He has no idea what's involved." She yanked a tall stem of red ginger out of the vase and clipped it, then tucked the ginger back into the arrangement. Now it was too short.

Mele watched, a smile tugging at the corners of her lips. Luana glanced at her, then back at her flower arrangement. Then she laughed. She removed the offending ginger, poking it back into a bucket of mixed flowers on the table beside her.

"Okay."

She set the almost-completed arrangement in the center of her table and stepped back.

"Let me put this aside for a while, before I *really* wreck it. You want to have a Popsicle?" She turned to Mele, eyebrows raised to emphasize her question.

"Sure. It'll be like old times."

Luana walked to the front of the store where a small freezer beside the entry was stocked with ice cream treats. When they were little, Mele would walk to the store with Luana after school and they would share a Popsicle. Orange or cherry, never grape. Popsicles no longer came double, but they could still share the camaraderie while indulging in individual treats.

Luana took two narrow paper-wrapped packages from the freezer and held them up for Mele to see. "Cherry?"

"Great."

Together, they headed toward the back of the store, walking out the rear door. Down three steps and across a narrow lawn stood the Young residence. A stone bench squatted against the retaining wall alongside the steps, and Luana and Mele automatically turned toward it and sat. The view of the old house was softened by the extensive flower gardens, the basis of Luana's business. Red and pink ginger, ti leaves, smaller varieties of heliconia, anthuriums sheltered by *hapu* tree ferns—the masses of color made a cheerful setting for an afternoon break.

Luana tore the paper from her Popsicle, crushing the wrapper and pushing it into the pocket of her shorts. Mele did the same.

"Umm," Mele said, taking a lick of the cold, flavored ice. "This is good. It's hot this afternoon."

She stuck her legs straight out in front of her, leaning back until her shoulders could rest against the lava rock that made up the retaining wall. "So, tell me more about this guy. I think it sounds romantic, his wanting to get married so quickly."

"Oh, no, you don't understand at all."

Luana's frustration was evident in her voice, causing Mele to glance at her with a startled expression. It just went to show how much Jake had changed her life, Luana thought. Her best friend was looking at her like she was nuts.

"*He* isn't the one getting married," Luana explained. "He wants me to make the arrangements for a female relative of his. He hasn't specified just what the relationship is though. And he won't tell me her name or the name of the groom. Calls them Mr. and Mrs. Smith."

Luana didn't share the fact that he'd slipped once and called the bride by her first name. She'd promised the hotel—and indirectly, Jake—discretion, and she kept her promises.

Mele snorted a laugh and Luana nodded at her.

"My sentiment exactly. Anyway, he says that he'll make all the decisions, and pay all the bills, so why am I concerned?"

Mele stared. "You're kidding, right?"

"Oh, no." Luana bit off a bit of ice and shook her head at Mele while it melted in her mouth. "Let me tell you, some of these people are just plain crazy. I didn't believe it before I took this job. But now I'm convinced. Just last week I got a call from some idiot who wanted to get married topless. She said she wanted a really authentic old style Hawaiian wedding, and didn't that mean no top?"

Mele was laughing. "And did you arrange it for her?"

"No way. I told her the Kukui Wana'ao was a sophisticated resort and wouldn't condone a half-naked bride." She grinned. "But I phrased it in a most proper and respectful fashion." It was her turn to laugh. "I may also have let drop a reference to the State of Hawaii's decency laws. Delicately, of course."

"Of course." Mele laughed. "So why don't you use the same story on this other guy? You know, this is a classy resort, we can't plan a wedding for a mystery guest."

Luana licked her Popsicle. Her eyes stared into the plants fronting the house, masses of colored crotons and ti leaves with froths of ferns at their base. But she didn't see the glorious golds and greens and pinks of the leaves and fronds. Instead, she was seeing Jake's smile. Practiced or not, it was one attractive grin.

She shook her head to rid it of Jake's handsome face. He might be handsome, but he was also a nuisance.

"It's not that easy. The general manager called me in before he arrived and said this was an important guest and I should see to it that his plans were taken care of."

Luana could see Mele's eyes widen as she thought this over.

"Wow. He must be some important guy." Mele's voice was awed. "Is he someone famous?"

"No. I'm sure not." Luana was suddenly flustered. "Anyway, I've never heard of him."

Luana's tongue flicked out over the Popsicle, enjoying the sweet coldness of it and trying to think of a way to explain Jake's charm to Mele. "It's hard to explain about this guy. He's . . . charming—I guess that's the word I want. He could be a politician."

"Maybe that's it." Mele sat up straight, excitement visible in every part of her body. "Maybe he's a political assistant for some big politician, arranging a wedding for some important guy and that's why they want to keep it a secret."

"Yeah, sure." Luana laughed. "Maybe Ray Hamada is getting married," she said, mentioning the name of a local politician who was often listed among the Islands' most eligible bachelors.

Mele's expression suddenly saddened. "You think so? That would be an awful shame. I wonder who the lucky gal could be."

Luana stared at her friend. "Mele, for gosh sakes. You don't even know him. It's not as if you have a chance of marrying the man. And anyway, we're just speculating here. The guy at the hotel is a *haole*. He's a real stylish dresser, and has the bluest eyes you've ever seen. He might work for a mainland politician, but I doubt if he would be an important assistant to a local guy."

No, Luana thought. Jake Lawrence's appearance screamed money and power. She had him pegged as a very successful businessman. With his looks, if he was a politician, she would bet she and Mele would have heard of him. For one thing, he would easily have made the magazines' "sexiest men alive" lists; the most attractive politicians always did. And, Luana thought with a smile, Mele was intimately familiar with those lists.

Mele cheered up. "Yeah, you're right. Maybe it's not even a politician. It could be a big celebrity—a rock star or something."

Luana laughed so suddenly, she began to cough. "Yeah, right. Maybe it's Madonna."

Mele laughed too as she summarily dismissed Luana's proposal. "She already got married."

The fact that she didn't know this, didn't bother Luana at all. "She did? Well, Britney Spears then."

Luana looked over at Mele. "Is she even old enough to get married?" She shrugged, obviously not worried by her lack of knowledge when it came to pop stars. "You know I don't keep up with all these rock stars."

"Well, I like to. I always watch those entertainment shows they have on TV. They're interesting, I think. I like to see how the other half lives. My nieces keep me up on the younger groups." Mele scrunched her nose. "They are into the boy bands big time. There are a bunch of them, and you should see these guys. They all look alike to me, but my nieces can go on for hours about each of the guys and who's the best-looking. It's unbelievable. Were we ever like that?"

Luana shrugged. She knew what Mele meant. She had a preteen niece too. It was how she knew about Britney Spears. "I doubt it. We were into hula big time, remember, so we didn't have as much time for some of this other stuff. All our spare time went into dance."

"My nieces don't do much except watch TV and play computer games. I tried to get them interested in dancing, but didn't have any luck. And my brother says he doesn't want to have to take them into Kona or Kamuela every weekend for lessons. And I have to work on the weekends, so I can't do it either."

"Maybe you should give them some lessons yourself," Luana suggested.

Mele didn't look enthused by the prospect. "I don't know. That would be like trying to teach your sister. No respect for a relative, you know? I'm not sure it would work out too well."

"Maybe you're right."

Luana crushed the last bit of red ice between her teeth and stood. "I guess we both ought to get back to work." She heaved a large sigh. "If I'm going to get this mysterious wedding done in a manner to make the Kukui Wana'ao proud, I have to get busy. I'll check my lists tonight—once I finish that flower arrangement. Make sure I haven't forgotten anything."

"Okay. I need to get back too, to start setting up for the early birds. Thanks for the Popsicle."

While Luana shrugged off her thanks, Mele stood and stretched, throwing her arms high above her head. Then she straightened her blouse and followed Luana to the steps leading back to the store.

"I don't know why you're letting this whole thing bother you, Luana. Just do whatever the guy says, and don't worry about it."

Luana paused, one foot on the top step, one on the stair below. Her forehead wrinkled as she tried to puzzle out her dilemma.

"I guess I could. I don't know why I'm having such a hard time with it. I think it's his attitude that irritates me. He thinks he's so handsome and charming. He has this smile. It's just so practiced-looking, you know? I can almost see him rehearsing in his shaving mirror every morning."

Plus, I'm mad that I let him get to me, Luana added to herself as she finished climbing the stairs. Because there was no denying that she was attracted to Jake. And even with the web of secrecy around him, she was aware that he was completely unsuitable for her.

Luana's assessment of Jake seemed to pique Mele's interest. "Handsome and charming, huh? And is he?"

"Yeah, he is." Luana frowned. "I just can't help thinking that he's using that smile and those dimples to distract me. To get his way, you know?"

"Hmm, dimples too." Mele grinned. "I'd say you're distracted all right."

Luana's frown deepened. "No, it's more that I'm irritated," she insisted.

"Well, whatever," Mele answered with a laugh.

They'd reached the back of the store, and Mele gestured toward Luana's worktable, still covered with buckets of cut flowers, and the one partially completed arrangement.

"You go on and finish mangling your flower arrangements." She gave her friend a quick hug and flashed an impudent grin. "I'll see you tomorrow. I want to hear more about this charming *haole.*"

Mele almost skipped through the store, waving to Mr. and Mrs. Young on her way through. They returned the greeting, though they were both busy with customers. Luana didn't wave, but she knew they made note of her return. A friend had once asked her if she found it stifling, having her parents so close by all the time. But she found their attention and concern comforting.

Luana returned to her flower arrangements. It took twice the time it usually did for her to finish the vases to her satisfaction. Thoughts of Jake continued to distract her. She replayed their luncheon conversation, thought again of everything they'd talked about. She recalled what she'd said to him, reworded sentences in her head. She wished she was sophisticated and witty, like some of the tourists she saw at the resort.

Then she scolded herself for such disloyal thoughts. She'd always been happy in little Malino, proud of her Island heritage. She could not let a handsome *haole* tourist disrupt her world. He would be gone in four weeks; there was no reason for him to stay once the wedding was over.

Luana's heart suddenly plunged. Actually, there was no reason for him to stay once the wedding *plans* were complete. What did she actually know about Jake Lawrence and his plans?

Luana thought over what he'd revealed about himself over their lunch. Several minutes of intense contemplation provided the answer. Nothing. She knew what movies he liked, that he had eclectic taste in music. She knew that he liked the Islands and was beginning to enjoy his vacation. But she didn't know where he lived or what he did for a living. Except, of course, that it must be something lucrative. Otherwise, he would not be a very important client of the Kukui Wana'ao Resort.

Finally she placed the completed arrangements in the walk-in refrigerator. She'd deliver them to the offices in the morning before she reported to her job at the resort. Before she saw Jake again.

Jake, meanwhile, spent a pleasant but lonely evening at the resort. He ate a late dinner at the Terrace Restaurant so that he could listen to the musical act Luana had recommended. And tortured himself with thoughts of the lovely wedding coordinator.

He had ample chance to hook up with other women. Flirty glances were thrown his way, but Jake simply was not interested. The deeply tanned or sunburned mainland women in their designer resort wear just could not compare with the golden-skinned Island beauty in her conservative muumuu who refused to leave his mind. There was something about Luana that appealed to him. Perhaps it was her serious concentration on business, or her sense of fun when relaxing. One thing he was sure of—Luana Young was the most interesting woman he'd met in a long time.

When he finally retreated to his room, Jake threw open the sliding doors on the balcony, got a soda from the room refrigerator, found a glass and some ice, and went to sit outside. The moon was a small crescent, high in a sky filled with stars. Sparkles of moonlight, perhaps even starlight, reflected off the rippling ocean waves. The beach below was rocky, not the smooth white sand most people envisioned when they thought of Hawaii. Like Jake himself before he arrived on the Big Island, Waikiki and the beautiful Maui beaches were what sprang to mind when the word beach was mentioned. But of course Waikiki and Maui were too popular and well known for Callie's wedding. Her celebrity required an out-of-the-way place. The relatively new Kukui Wana'ao Resort was perfect in that way. Certainly off the beaten track. He couldn't imagine any of the tabloids discovering their plans by accident. Or even by design.

Jake sipped his soda, refreshed by the cold, sweet liquid. It wasn't hot, but the heavy humidity took a toll. Far across the stretch of water before him, he could see the twinkling lights of another resort further along the coast. Out to sea was the lonely light of a single boat.

Jake watched the lights of the solitary boat as it moved slowly along the water. He'd never done much sailing or boating, but the idea suddenly appealed. Wouldn't it be fun to be out there right now, with Luana? Just the two of them, together on the vast ocean, looking up at the stars.

Jake sighed. He tried to turn his mind away from such fantasies, going inside to fetch a thriller he'd started reading on the beach that afternoon. It was a good tale; ordinarily, he would have found it gripping. But tonight, Jake preferred to stare at the ocean and think about a woman with a graceful walk and a tempting smile.

Finally, tired and still somewhat jet-lagged, Jake fell into bed, the sliding doors left open so that the sound of the waves could serve as his lullaby.

He felt as though he'd only been asleep for a moment when he was rudely awakened by the buzz of his cell phone.

Blinking in confusion as he fumbled for the phone, Jake noticed that the sky was lightening, but the sun was not yet up.

"Jake!" The cheerful female voice started speaking as soon as he said hello. "I just talked to Tommy about the wedding."

Jake glanced at the clock. Not even 6:00. He tried closing his eyes again. Maybe he was dreaming. He'd had trouble falling asleep, Luana's face and figure disturbing his peace of mind. It didn't feel like he'd been asleep all that long.

But the phone in his hand felt all too real. Cold, hard plastic pressed against his fingers, against his right ear.

"Callie. Do you know what time it is?"

"Sure."

The perky voice carried clearly into his ear canal. His half-sister was obviously in a cheerful mood today.

"It's almost noon. We didn't perform last night, so I got up early."

Jake sighed. "Callie. *There* it's almost noon. Here, the sun hasn't even come up yet. And I'm supposed to be on vacation," he added in a resigned voice.

"Aw, poor Jake. I'm sorry, big brother. I forgot about the time difference. I guess you wanted to sleep in, huh?"

Jake sighed again. Callie was definitely in a good mood. The tour must be going well.

"Are you getting a chance to relax, Jake?" Concern now laced her voice.

Jake knew he had to forgive her. She was in love. How could he expect her to remember the six-hour time difference?

"Yeah, I'm trying to relax. I've been swimming and sunbathing. Finally had a chance to begin the latest Tom Clancy."

"That's nice."

In the misty light of the predawn, Jake had to smile. Callie could be so narrowly focused, she probably didn't even know what he was talking about when he mentioned Tom Clancy. But hadn't she mentioned the wedding?

"So . . . you talked to Tommy?"

Callie's voice brightened. Jake knew she was smiling.

"He just called. They're in Boston."

Jake could hear the wistful quality in her voice. She was in Atlanta. When Callie had announced her intention to marry Tommy Teague of Four-by-Six, she claimed to be deeply in love. Jake had wondered. Was she really in love, or just thrilled that Tommy had proposed? Tommy was the most popular member of Four-by-Six, named one of the country's most eligible bachelors in a recent celebrity magazine poll.

Jake smiled. He didn't have to wonder any longer. He could hear the love in her voice when she talked about Tommy. That was pure longing in her voice when she mentioned the distance between them. He was beginning to feel better about the marriage, even though she was awfully young.

Jake tuned in to her dialogue just in time.

"We talked about the wedding, so I thought I'd better call and let you know."

"That was a good idea." Since they'd left it all to him.

"It's so great of you to do all this for us, Jake."

"It's okay." Jake was resigned to waking up now. He pushed the covers aside and piled the pillows behind his head. "So what did you decide that you wanted to tell me about?"

"Oh, this is so neat!"

Jake had to smile to hear the excitement in her voice.

"You know Monroe Johnston?"

Jake made a noise in his throat to acknowledge that he did. Monroe was one of the guys who made up the Four part of Four-by-Six. The others were Michael Lee, Ross Knight, and Tommy Teague. The Six in their name stood for the six musicians who backed them up.

"Well, Monroe's father is a preacher." Callie almost squealed the final word. "Isn't that cute? That's what he calls him. A preacher."

"I think it's a Southern thing," Jake murmured.

"Yeah, could be. They're from north Georgia, you know."

Callie might not have the education he wished for her, but she did know her geography. Touring had given her a practical education in it. It was one of the reasons he was surprised at her for forgetting the time difference. She was usually better at time zones than he was.

Callie continued to chatter. "Reverend Johnston is coming to the show tonight. I left a backstage pass out front for him so he can come back to meet me after the show. He told Monroe that he'd be proud to marry Tommy and me. Isn't that great?"

Jake was wide awake now, and glad to hear Callie getting excited about the wedding. He just hoped she wouldn't start taking a big interest and interfere in choices he'd already made for her. *He* didn't care if she changed everything, but he didn't think he could handle facing Luana and telling her they would have to start all over. It made him shudder just thinking of the disappointment he would see in her eyes.

"And does the Reverend Johnston know that the whole thing has to be kept quiet?"

Jake swore he could hear the frown in Callie's voice.

"Of course. Honestly, Jake, his own son has the same kind of problems Tommy and I have. Of course he knows better than to tell anyone."

Jake just lay on his rumpled bed and grinned at her outrage.

"You're right. I'm sorry, Callie. I guess I haven't done enough unwinding. I've been going full tilt for the last two years, and this is my first vacation. You can't expect me to relax right off. I have to ease into it." He couldn't resist adding, "And I didn't get enough sleep last night."

Callie was prompt with another apology. "I'm sorry, Jake. I guess you do need some time to ease into a vacation." She didn't sound certain, but she agreed with good grace.

"So, is the wedding all set?"

"Pretty much. You have no idea how much is involved in planning a wedding, Callie." Okay, so he couldn't resist whining a little. She had stuck him with this job, and he was entitled.

"I know a lot is involved, Jake. But you're so good at all that micro-managing stuff. Besides, you needed a rest so badly, and you wouldn't listen to any of us when we suggested a vacation."

Jake heard it, but could hardly believe Callie's blithe remark. She'd *planned* this?

"I don't recall you suggesting a vacation."

"Of course you don't. You never hear things you don't agree with." Her voice was matter-of-fact. "And you never like to let anyone decide what you're going to do either. But Dad and I both suggested you take some time off— more than once. Besides, you've been working so hard for so long you think you're indispensable."

"And I'm not." Jake was beginning to grin.

"Of course not. Almost, but not quite," she added with a laugh.

Jake laughed too, but he wasn't finding this conversation as humorous as she was.

"You didn't set this up just to get me to take a vacation, did you? You do plan to get married?"

"Of course!"

Her reply was fast and loud. Jake pulled the phone away from his ear for a moment.

"Callie." His voice softened. "Are you sure you don't want to get more involved in planning this wedding? I'm meeting with the coordinator later this morning to finalize plans. You could still make decisions about food and flowers and all those dozens of other things."

"I'm sure you're doing a great job, Jake. And I really don't have the time."

Her answer didn't surprise Jake, but he was disappointed. Until he remembered that that meant he would continue his close association with Luana, planning those dozens of details. His lips curved into a smile.

"Oh, there is one thing, Jake. We were all watching *The Sound of Music* the other day. Did you know the big thing in England these days is to watch a sing-along version of *The Sound of Music?*"

"I've heard that. There's a sing-along version of *Mary Poppins* too."

"Oh, yeah? Well, we didn't have the sing-along version of *The Sound of Music,* but we decided since we were cooped up in the hotel, we'd do our own sing-along with the DVD. It was lots of fun."

"That's nice." Jake was beginning to wonder if she was leading up to something. Didn't she begin by saying she had decided on something for the wedding?

"Well, we were having a great time, singing along. And you know the scene where Julie Andrews gets married?"

Ah, finally. He recalled a beautiful scene in an old cathedral, Julie Andrews walking up the aisle, and yards and yards of white drapery. Good grief, he hoped she didn't want a twenty-foot train! Or was that the woman's veil that trailed so far behind her?

"Well, you know that music they play when she walks in the church? The girls thought that might be a good song to use when I walk in. I called Stacey to get her opinion and she liked it too."

What a relief.

"Great. I knew you wouldn't go for Wagner's 'Bridal Chorus'."

"If that's the old 'Here Comes the Bride,' then you'd better believe it."

Her reply brought a smile to Jake's lips.

"I'd been thinking about 'Also Sprach Zarathustra,' but I guess it wouldn't really be appropriate. But wouldn't it have been great to come in to that? So dramatic." She heaved a theatrical sigh.

Jake had to agree that the Strauss would have certainly been dramatic.

"It's your wedding, Callie. You use whatever music you want."

"Well, I want it to be nice too. Especially now that we have Reverend Johnston." But her serious voice turned mischievous when she continued. "But I want something totally funky to walk out with. Maybe 'Celebration,' you know? Don't you think that would be appropriate?"

Jake laughed. "If that's what you want. And I do think it's appropriate. A wedding should be fun, Callie, but you're right. The ceremony is the serious part. And I think it's great that you have the Reverend Johnston to take charge of that."

"Me too. It was great talking to you, Jake, but I have to go. The tour has been great—we're getting the best crowds. But I can hardly wait for it to be over so that we can join you there and get married."

Jake wished her good-bye, passing on good wishes for the other members of the touring group. Callie had asked all three of her backup singers to be attendants. It might seem logical to outside observers, but with Callie nothing could be assumed. He'd been proud of her for asking them. When she was on her best behavior, like she was this morning, she was a joy to be around. It was a shame that "superstar Callie" had to rear her ugly head sometimes.

Jake lay against the piled-up pillows and closed his eyes. Maybe he could get in another hour of sleep. But Luana's face seemed imprinted on the backs of his eyelids. And Callie's voice still echoed through his mind. His lips began to twitch as he thought how happy Luana would be to learn he had information directly from the bride. He could see her smile now. . . .

He finally gave up; he wasn't going to get any more sleep. He was seeing Luana later this morning anyway. He'd agreed to stop by her office about 10:00. He glanced at the clock. Still almost four hours away.

He threw off the bedclothes and got out of bed. He'd go for a long swim in the cool morning water. It seemed like the best option.

Chapter Five

Jake thought he saw Luana at her desk when he passed by on his way back to his room. The water had been refreshingly cold, and he'd swum until he was worn out, but it did little toward excising Luana from his mind. Hair wet and dripping, a towel wrapped around his waist, Jake peeked around the edge of the door.

After a night of reminiscences and dreams, he had not conjured her up now. There she was, sitting at her desk, peering at the screen of her computer. Her face appeared lit with an otherworldly glow, and her gorgeous eyes were fixed in concentration, a faint wrinkle marring the expanse of her forehead.

Jake could tell when she spotted him. Her head moved away from the monitor and was once more just a face lit by the room's harsh artificial lights. Her eyes widened, then the doe-in-the-headlights look slowly changed to a smile;

it started at her lips and spread gradually over the rest of her face until it sparkled from her eyes.

Jake felt his breath catch in his throat. Luana's smiles were hard on his peace of mind. He began to wonder if he should return to his room, or head back to the cold pool for a few more laps.

Instead, his legs decided for him, moving of their own volition into her open door.

"You're here early."

Luana checked her watch, then looked up at him with a smile. "I'm an early riser. And I wanted to have all my notes organized and ready for our meeting later."

Luana stood, rising politely, he assumed, since he was standing.

"What are you doing up so early? Is your body still on Eastern time?" She gave him a sympathetic smile.

Jake stepped fully into the room, readjusting the towel wrapped around his waist. He might have a modest pair of trunks underneath, but he would feel odd standing before her in swim trunks when she was covered from neck to ankle by her dress. It seemed strange enough standing there bare-chested. And now that he was inside, the artificially cooled air was making him feel chilled.

"No. I'm from California. I got a phone call this morning from someone in the East, though. Someone who forgot there's a six-hour time difference in the summer," he added with a wry smile.

Luana laughed. "Lucky you."

It was easy to laugh with her, even though the skin on his arms was beginning to roughen into the characteristic bumps of goose flesh.

"Why don't I run upstairs and change before I turn into an icicle. Then I can come back for our meeting. Might as well get it out of the way, since we're both here, then you can have the rest of your day for . . . whatever."

Jake smiled at her. His best smile, the one that turned mainland women to mush, but seemed to have no effect on Luana. Jake watched with interest as her eyes locked on his mouth. Well, up till now she had seemed impervious to it. His smile grew wider as Luana swallowed. The tip of her tongue darted out of her mouth and ran quickly across the lower edge of her upper lip.

It was Jake's turn to swallow. What exciting lips Luana had. He couldn't look at them without imaging what it would be like to kiss them. He could almost taste them. Luana's lips would be soft and sweet. Not sickly sweet, like pure honey, but flavored with some exotic seasoning. Hibiscus, maybe, or jasmine. She didn't seem to wear perfume, so he didn't know why he associated jasmine with her. But he did. It seemed the perfect scent for her, spicy and tropical. Unusual. Exotic. Like Luana herself.

And while hibiscus didn't have a scent, he'd admired the large colorful blooms he'd seen in abundance in the resort gardens. They belonged in the lush tropical surroundings, just as Luana did. He'd been given some hibiscus tea once, by a client; he hadn't enjoyed it at the time, yet the flowery taste came back to him now, the perfect sweetness for an island flower like Luana.

Jake shook himself free of his fanciful thoughts and pulled his eyes away from Luana's lips. She appeared embarrassed and he scolded himself; he must have been staring and made her uncomfortable. He'd better watch his manners; his mama would be ashamed of him.

"I'll go on and get dressed."

To his chagrin, Luana turned pink at his words.

"I'll be back in . . ." He glanced down, meaning to check

his watch. Then he realized he wasn't wearing his watch. He met Luana's gaze with a small shrug. "Let's say twenty minutes. How's that?"

"Fine."

Luana managed to get the one word out without embarrassing herself further. As soon as Jake left, she sat down in her chair and bent her head, almost hiding behind her computer. She'd never been so mortified as when he'd caught her staring at his mouth. Really, the man had the nicest mouth. His lips were neither thin nor full, but seemed just right for kissing. There was something about the way they twitched at the corners, like he was always ready to share a smile. He probably tasted good too, like the best coffee. She didn't know why coffee came to mind when she thought of him, but it seemed appropriate. Maybe because he dressed the way she imagined the young mainland professionals would—the ones who crowded coffee bars like the one on "Friends."

Thinking about it now made Luana turn pink all over again. She couldn't seem to help herself when it came to Jake. There was something about the man that sent all her good intentions sailing away on the outgoing tides. She'd determined to be all business with him, treat him like the important client he was, and nothing more. And then she'd seen him standing there in her doorway, wearing nothing but a wet towel. His chest was broad with a sprinkling of pale brown hairs and already showing the effects of the island sun. His hair dripped short curls over his forehead and water over her carpet. But he looked so sweet, she'd wanted to rush across the room and wrap him in her arms. Share her warmth with him. He'd looked cold.

Luana sighed. So much for good intentions.

* * *

Jake slipped back into the room approximately twenty minutes later, as promised. With him he carried a tray laden with a coffeepot, cups, and a napkin-lined basket.

"I thought you might enjoy a little something."

He deposited the tray on her desk, then with a deft movement he uncovered a cache of golden-brown sweet rolls hidden in the napkin-lined basket. "Voila."

Luana stared at the insulated pot, the china cups, at the rolls enclosed in the linen napkin. She didn't know what to say. Why did he have to be so nice just when she'd made a firm resolve to keep her distance?

Jake, watching her, frowned. "What's the matter? Not hungry?"

Luana could hear the hesitation in his voice. If she wasn't mistaken, he was hurt that she wasn't showing her appreciation for his gift.

Luana attempted a smile.

"I'm just surprised. However did you manage to get room service to respond so quickly?"

"I called as soon as I got upstairs. Was that quick? This *is* a five-star resort, remember."

Jake's smile could light her office without the aid of any lamps, Luana thought.

"I don't usually eat breakfast."

"That's not good for you, you know. It's important to start out the day with some fuel for the system." Jake shook his head sadly from side to side. "I always eat breakfast. And I haven't had any yet. You aren't going to make me eat alone, are you?"

He lifted one of the rolls. "Look at that now. Isn't it beautiful? A perfect roll. Nicely browned on top and still warm. They said they were Portuguese sweet bread rolls."

Luana looked at the big grin he flashed her way. She let out a long breath.

"That is a very lovely roll."

Jake waved the pastry in front of her face.

"Smell that wonderful aroma. Nothing like the smell of fresh bread, is there?" He replaced the roll in its basket and reached for two small containers. "And here we have butter and honey." He picked up a miniature glass jar and peered at the label. "And guava jelly."

Luana laughed. "Okay, okay. I'll have a roll."

Jake's grin widened as he proffered the basket, allowing her to select one of the rolls. Then he poured two cups of coffee, handing one to her along with a little pitcher of milk. "One Kona coffee, with milk. Right?"

Luana's brows rose. "That's right." She accepted the cup with what seemed to her a very awkward motion. Her face had burned with the first scent of coffee. Her earlier fantasies coming back to haunt her, she thought, remembering her notion of kissing Jake and how he might taste. Now, he would most certainly taste of coffee. And possibly jam and honey. They both would.

She stared at the cup and saucer in one hand, the roll in the other. She quickly lowered the cup and saucer to her desk, flustered. Then she accepted the pitcher of cream with what she hoped was a normal smile of thanks.

"I'm impressed. You remembered how I take my coffee from our one lunch together?"

"What can I say?" His smile was boyishly charming. "I'm a man of many sterling qualities."

Luana laughed, almost choking on her first bite. She followed it quickly with a sip of coffee. Now she had a scorched tongue to go with the scratchy throat.

"Ah, shall we get to work? While we eat?"

She'd love to enjoy a casual half hour with him while they ate. They would chat and laugh and have a good time. But she was trying her best to keep him at a distance, to keep things on a business basis. For her own sanity. Yet how could she continue to do it when he did sweet things like bringing her breakfast and remembering how she liked her coffee?

She watched Jake as he stood beside the desk. He'd already finished off one roll, and was replenishing his coffee. But even as he performed these physical tasks, she could almost see him debating his next action. Sit at her desk and work with her on the wedding, or try to jolly her into having more of his impromptu breakfast? He hesitated, then moved around to sit in the chair beside her desk.

"Okay. Where were we?"

Relieved, Luana finished the roll and sipped from her coffee cup.

"First, *mahalo* for the breakfast, Jake. That was very good."

Luana ducked her head as she shuffled some papers on her desk. She might be a grown woman, but she began to act like a teenager when Jake was around. A starstruck teenager. *Remember puppy love, Luana?* she asked herself. Tall, handsome Danny Higashi her junior year in high school. She'd cried for days when she learned he'd asked Angie Tau to the prom. Then promptly gotten over it when John Akana asked her. John wasn't as good-looking, and he wasn't on the basketball team, but he'd turned out to be a much better match for her. Danny had definitely been a crush—puppy love.

That's what you've got here. An attractive, well-to-do haole man comes along and looks at you like you're something special—and you fall for it right away. Grow up, girl!

If there's anything you don't need complicating your life, it's a brief romance with a tourist.

Strengthened by her internal lecture, Luana moved and clicked the mouse, keeping her eyes fixed on the screen. She would not meet Jake's amazing blue eyes, or glance at his firm lips, moving as he chewed another roll. And she definitely would not look at his competent hands, lightly tanned now from his time in the tropical sun. Or at the way his fingers curled around the curve of the cup to lift it, rather than doing the ordinary thing and inserting them through the handle.

Luana cleared her throat.

"Now . . ."

Her eyes remained on the computer screen, but Luana was still seeing strong hands with no-nonsense nails. Clipped, not bitten. Hands that would look light next to her skin.

The thought of his hand on her arm made Luana shiver.

Jake was instantly solicitous. "Are you cold? Shall I re-fresh your coffee?" He was already lifting the pot as his last words were spoken.

Luana shook her head, afraid of what her rebelling mind might conjure if he came around the desk to refill her cup. Then, changing her mind since she really did want more, she hastily picked up the saucer and handed it across the desk.

While Jake poured, Luana finally channeled her mind toward business.

"I have our nicest room scheduled for your reception. Uh, your relative's reception." She accepted her refilled cup with a nod of thanks, setting it to her right, before the computer monitor. "As to the ceremony itself, there are several options. We can do something in the lobby beside the waterfall, or there are a number of spots outdoors that are popular."

"No."

His reply was so quick, so vehement, Luana fumbled the cup she had just begun to lift, spilling coffee out into the saucer. She looked up in surprise.

Jake raked his fingers through his hair. Darn, but he was going to get himself in trouble. Memories of his pleasant conversation with Callie earlier that morning flew to the back of his mind. Irritation with her returned—irritation that he'd finally met a woman he really liked; irritation that his sister's celebrity was hampering his chance at a relationship with her.

As he took a napkin from the tray and leaned over to soak up the overflow from Luana's saucer, he swore softly at the situation he found himself in. He'd never wanted to plan Callie's wedding, but here he was, doing it anyway.

"Ah, I'm sorry. I didn't mean to startle you. It just surprised me that you would have something as private as a wedding in a public area like the lawn or the lobby."

He hoped his voice was steady. Normal. The need for secrecy was essential. Not being up-front with Luana was making it difficult. But it was Callie's decision not to tell anyone except the resort general manager. It would be hard enough to manage once she arrived on the scene. So right now, he couldn't explain his concerns about public areas. He'd have to rely on the fact that a wedding was a family affair. It seemed to him that even a normal couple might object to having their wedding in an area that was open to the public.

Luana answered, as though his question was a normal concern for a person planning a wedding. "Both areas are popular for weddings. We can rope off the lobby alongside the waterfall. The couple stands there, before the waterfall, which makes an attractive backdrop for the wedding photos. The chairs for the guests are set up alongside the garden. It's not as open as you think."

Luana lifted her cup and took a sip of the cooling coffee. "Actually, your party may be too large for the lobby. It works best with small groups."

Jake was glad to hear it, but didn't comment.

"As for the lawn, well, there are several options. We held a dozen weddings outside last year. A tent can be erected if there's a concern about rain or sun. Or even just for privacy. But our lawns and gardens are very beautiful, and there are several spots that are off the usual paths, and therefore very private."

Luana met his gaze across the desk. It made it difficult for him to think, and he had to concentrate on her words. The sound of her voice alone was almost like music. But listening to tone and rhythm wasn't enough—he needed to hear the lyrics.

"The most popular outdoor site is right alongside the ocean. It's a beautiful corner of the property, with a wide lawn for setting up the chairs, and a lovely floral garden that serves as backdrop where the couple can exchange their vows. It's alongside the golf course, but far enough away that rogue balls are not a problem. It's especially beautiful for sunset weddings like yours."

Luana finished with a smile. A lovely smile, true, but Jake was determined to have the ceremony inside.

"Isn't there a room we can use? Why can't we have it in the same room where we'll have the reception?"

Jake had a feeling he'd just asked a stupid question. Not that Luana said anything, but he felt he was getting good at reading her body language. And that last question must be one that could be included in a book called *Weddings for Dumbbells.*

"The reception room will be set up for dinner and dancing. There will be a head table for the wedding party, slightly raised, so that everyone in the room will be able to see them. The ceremony requires rows of seats, with an aisle up the middle."

Then, as if he didn't already feel like a real idiot, she elaborated.

"Like a church."

"Hmm. How about an adjacent room? Then the guests could go right from the ceremony to the reception next door. Quick and easy."

That sounded good to Jake. It seemed like it would make everything easier for everyone.

"You're using one of the ballrooms, right? Two hundred people can't be using the entire room. So you could section off another part of it for the ceremony."

"I can check," Luana told him.

He could see that she had problems with his scenario. He quickly learned why.

"There is usually a down time between the ceremony and the reception. It's when pictures of the wedding party are done. And of the couple with their relatives. Then, when the couple leaves the ceremony to go to the reception hall is when you have the various good-luck traditions. You know, throwing rice, or confetti, or birdseed. Or blowing bubbles. Some people even release butterflies or white doves. Of course, that couldn't be done indoors," she added.

Jake's mind was boggling at all this new information. Of course he knew about throwing rice. But birdseed? Bubbles? Butterflies?

"And then there's the receiving line. If you want to have one, it will have to be outside the room used for the ceremony, or inside the reception hall. If you have it at the reception, the wedding party and the parents of the bride and groom would line up and greet everyone as they come in."

Luana looked at Jake expectantly.

Jake shook his head, an ironic grin twisting his mouth. "I just keep learning more and more that I don't know. I'll have to think about the receiving line, but we probably won't have one. And I'll make a decision later on the bubbles or birdseed. But could you check on the availability of another room?"

Luana's gaze returned to the computer. He assumed she was checking the availability of the banquet rooms for the wedding date. Maybe he should attempt to find a church. But although Callie had a minister to perform the ceremony, Jake found it hard to imagine her walking down the aisle of a church. Callie was so brash and irreverent. A church demanded dignity and reserve. Though he had to admit she had chosen a beautiful—and traditional—piece of music for her entrance.

Actually, the seaside would have been the perfect place for Callie's wedding. She would have loved the sunset wedding Luana described. If she was plain Callie Lawrence and not "the" Callie Law. There was just no way to secure the area around the beach. He could see it now—boats of paparazzi bobbing offshore, the huge telephoto lenses flashing reflected light. Photographers hiding in the shrubbery. Helicopters overhead.

No, it would never do.

Luana looked up from the computer screen. He loved the

way she tilted her head to the side when she looked at him. Just as she was doing now.

"If I move you over to our largest ballroom, I'll have two rooms large enough. We could set one up with a low platform, a trellis, lots of fresh flowers, chairs for one hundred fifty to two hundred. It will be expensive."

Jake nodded. "That's fine."

They worked out a few more details, including the lighting and the types of plants and flowers that would give the illusion of a garden in the impersonal ballroom.

"Try to include some fragrant flowers," Jake suggested. "Callie likes strongly scented flowers."

"Mmm. Perhaps I can get some ginger. Ginger has a wonderful fragrance. Brings the tropics right into the room."

She pursed her lips as she stared into space, thinking. "That being the case, she might like a *pikake* and *maile* lei. Both *pikake* and *maile* have strong distinctive scents. *Pikake* is traditional for the bride, though she could wear both if she wanted to. *Maile* is traditional for the groom."

"Would she still carry a bouquet if she wore a lei? I'm sure she wouldn't want to miss having a bouquet."

To his delight, Luana smiled. Finally, he'd asked a proper question.

"Certainly she'd have a bouquet. I could arrange something that would coordinate. In fact, a thick *pikake* lei would look lovely with her strapless gown. She could wear it in place of jewelry. Her attendants can do the same, but with yellow ginger."

Jake watched Luana's face, animated by her excitement over the floral choices.

"It's also usual for the bride to have a separate, smaller, bouquet for throwing."

"So she doesn't throw the bouquet she carries through the ceremony, you mean?"

Luana nodded.

"Sure, if that's how it's usually done."

They discussed the food, music for the reception, flowers for the tables, and the wedding cake. Luana explained the various types of good luck customs. Rice, birdseed, confetti were all dismissed as inappropriate for the indoors. So too the white doves and butterflies.

"Too bad. I'll bet Callie would have loved the butterflies," Jake commented.

Luana smiled sympathetically. "Bubbles are very popular, and it's quite a sight when you have dozens of people blowing bubbles over the happy couple."

Jake could picture that. It would be nice. And Callie would never know about the butterflies if he didn't tell her.

Jake thought they were finally done, but Luana looked up at him, biting on one corner of her lower lip.

"Is there something else?"

"There's another good-luck custom practiced here in the Islands. The folding of a thousand and one origami cranes."

Jake raised a brow, but didn't comment.

Luana explained. "In ancient Japan, it was believed that the crane lived for one thousand years, and that when cranes mated, they mated for life. For that reason, it became a symbol for good fortune and longevity in marriage. The thousand and one good luck cranes are a tradition that began in Hawaii, and has been adopted by all couples, not just those of Japanese-American ancestry. The extra crane is Hawaii's addition for good luck."

Luana was immersed in her story now, her hands gesturing before her as she spoke.

"Originally, it was said that the bride had to fold all one

thousand and one cranes herself so that she would learn patience, preparing herself for married life."

That was too much for Jake. His barking laugh startled Luana out of her tale, and for a moment she watched him, doubled over in his chair, eyes tearing from his laughter. Her scolding look just had him shaking his head.

Finally, he straightened, wiped his eyes with a handkerchief he took from a back pocket, and apologized.

"It's just . . . If you knew Callie . . ."

Another burst of laughter cut his statement short.

"She could stand to learn some patience all right, but I don't think making a thousand and one paper cranes would do it."

He blew his nose before continuing.

"However, please do go on. This is very interesting and I think Callie might actually want to do it."

So Luana resumed. "These days the bride usually receives assistance with the folding, from her friends and family, even from the groom. Then the paper cranes are mounted and framed to create a unique piece of art."

Luana pulled some brochures from her desk and pushed them across the desk to Jake.

"As you can see, the designs created can be almost anything, from these Japanese family crests called *mon,* to these scenic designs." Her graceful fingers indicated first one and then the other in the pamphlet illustrations. "The couple ends up with a lovely piece of framed artwork to hang in their home to remember their wedding day."

As she finished the explanation, Jake continued to stare at Luana. He loved watching her speak. She was really into weddings, that was obvious by the way she could become so passionate about these small details. But the good-luck cranes were something he felt Callie could get excited about. If he could catch her in a good mood to explain it.

So he nodded at Luana. "That sounds like something Callie would love. How would we do the cranes though?"

"I can arrange to have most of them made for you, but it would be nice if the bride could do a few herself. If you'd like, I can show you how to fold one. Then you can teach the bride, or we can just use the ones you make for good luck."

Jake didn't especially want to learn how to make origami cranes. But he did want to spend more time with Luana. And it didn't seem as if planning the wedding itself would require much more time. Her questions—hundreds of them, it seemed—must have covered everything by now.

So he agreed to learn.

Luana glanced quickly at her calendar.

"How about next week? I can leave a message in your room." She slanted a glance toward him. "Uh, you will be staying until the wedding?"

Was her voice hopeful? Jake ran searching eyes over her face. What he saw there made him smile. She was worried that he might be leaving the island! He'd bet on it. He was happy to reassure her.

"I'll be here. I'm supposed to be taking a long overdue vacation."

Luana smiled. "I can see you've been enjoying the sun."

"You mean the swim this morning?"

His questioning look made her elaborate.

She shook her head. "You're getting a tan. You were very pale when you first came to my office."

Luana reached out toward his face. Her long, graceful fingers hovered mere inches from his cheek. Jake was tempted to lean forward and touch his cheek to her fingers himself. But that would surely scare her away. Even now, she seemed to reconsider and pulled her hand quickly back.

"You look nice with a tan."

Luana looked at him shyly, her chin tipped down, her eyes slanted upward. "So, how do you feel about church music?"

Jake was at a loss. Didn't they decide to have the wedding in the hotel ballroom?

"Church music?"

Luana nodded. "You mentioned wanting to hear some local musical groups."

"Ahh. I do. I have no objection to going to church, if that's what you mean." *Especially if you're going to take me,* he thought. But he said, "Especially if the music is good."

"Great. Because I know just the place. Shall I pick you up out front around eight-thirty Sunday morning?"

"It's a date."

Chapter Six

"It's a date."

The words resonated through Luana's mind.

She was still hearing them later that afternoon in Malino, seeing the promise in Jake's eyes as he spoke. Luana had settled herself comfortably on a wooden bench just outside the entrance to the General Store. Changed into shorts and T-shirt, she crossed her legs in front of her and positioned a cardboard box full of vandas on her lap. At her feet, she put a large brown paper bag to catch the discarded outer petals.

She had to make two maunaloa-style vanda leis for an anniversary dinner that evening, which meant taking apart the blossoms so that she could string the dark trumpets without their light outer petals.

The front of the store was a fun place to work. Both pedestrians and General Store customers stopped to greet her, exchange a few words, and comment on her style of lei-making. Ten-year-old Jennie Aki stayed outside to help Luana disassemble the flowers while her mother shopped leisurely for some fabric. As they left, Laura Aki promised to call Luana with an order for flowers, she was so grateful for the quiet shopping time she had enjoyed.

Luana watched them leave with regret. She'd enjoyed the young girl's chatter. It just wasn't possible to languish over her own pseudo-relationship with Jake while sweet Jennie chatted about the cute new boy on her soccer team.

As she carefully plucked the dark centers of the orchids from the lighter petals surrounding it, Luana smiled in delight at her inspiration of settling outside the store to prepare her flowers for stringing. It was just the distraction she needed. She decided she would string the leis there as well.

Even with the interruptions, however, she found her mind jumping between the flowers, memories of her brief times with Jake, and the gossipy chatter with her neighbors.

She was grateful that the Sakumotos were traditionalists and preferred two matching vanda leis in the old maunaloa style. She could never have managed a cigar flower lei, if that had been the choice for Mr. Sakumoto. While the striped lei was particularly attractive on a man, stringing the hundreds of tiny cigar flowers would have taken more time than she now had. She was simply too distracted to do the careful placement necessary to achieve the striped effect.

As Luana began to feed the dark trumpets onto the long needle, she let her mind travel back over yesterday's luncheon with Jake. She'd had fun, she realized. She thought he had enjoyed their time together too. He was an interesting conversationalist, a man who knew how to make a woman feel at ease. She couldn't remember when she'd talked so much!

"Boy, have you got it bad."

Luana looked up to see Mele standing beside her.

"What are you talking about?" She continued feeding the dark orchid centers onto her needle.

"I came over to say hi because everyone's been telling me that you're out here stringing leis." Mele settled on the bench next to her friend, putting her hand into the box between them that held the flower centers. She took a handful, then gave them to Luana one by one to arrange on her needle. "But, Luana—you didn't even hear me say hello."

Luana shrugged. "I'm busy. And I have a lot on my mind too."

Mele just looked at her, continuing to pass the flowers to her. "So how's the secret wedding coming?"

"The secret wedding?" Luana laughed. "You make it sound so mysterious."

"Have you learned anything more about the bride and groom?"

"No."

"Then it *is* mysterious. How can any woman let some guy set up all the details of her wedding?"

Luana shrugged. "I've wondered the same thing. I think she must be young." She took a flower from Mele and placed it on the needle, then pushed all the pinned flowers into place on the string. "But I don't really know how they're doing it either. For all we know, he may be calling her every day, discussing every little detail with her."

"I still think it's odd."

Luana shrugged again. She thought it odd too, but she didn't want to make too big a point of it. She had to have some loyalty to her client.

"Everything is pretty well set for the wedding now. I still have to decide on the flowers. There will be a lot of them." Luana smiled at the thought of choosing so many flowers without the interference of the bride or either of the mothers. It was going to be a lot of fun.

She took another flower from Mele and pushed it onto the needle. "And I'm going to teach him to make paper cranes."

Mele laughed. "You're teaching *him* to make the cranes?"

Luana's shoulders rose up then dropped in a dismissive shrug. "Well, he's the only one here, isn't he? He says the bride likes the custom, and he'll teach her how to make them."

Mele talked on for another minute or two. Then, announcing that her break was over, she threw the flowers she still held into the box, and walked back to the restaurant where she worked.

Luana watched her go, realizing that she had probably driven her away without meaning to. But she didn't want to speculate about the mysterious bride whose wedding Jake was planning. It reminded her of how little she actually knew about Jake himself. For no matter how often she replayed their luncheon conversation in her mind, she realized that while she had spoken freely of her life outside the resort, he had said almost nothing about himself. While he now knew almost everything about her, she still didn't know what he did for a living, or exactly where on the mainland he lived. The small concession he'd made, telling her that he lived in California, was just that. A small concession. California was a big state. Obviously, the man had a thing for secrecy! Perhaps it ran in the family.

Luana frowned. She suspected the bride was quite young.

She couldn't imagine a mature woman giving up complete control of her own wedding. Most women began planning their weddings as children. She certainly had been thinking about her own wedding for years, even though she didn't have a steady boyfriend. And she remembered playing wedding as a child, using some old lace curtains of her mother's to fashion a "gown" and a veil.

There was just something about weddings. . . . Perhaps because they were the closest thing to fairy tales, yet they were fantasies that had a good chance of becoming reality.

Luana measured the length of strung flowers, flashing a smile of greeting at Mr. Jardine as he approached her bench. She quickly tied off the finished lei as he stopped to say hello. She would attach a bow to cover the knotted string when she finished the second.

"Is that for me?" Mr. Jardine shot her a flirty grin.

Luana had to smile. The man was seventy years old, at least. But he was a dear, and a familiar sight walking along the streets of Malino.

"Maybe next time, Mr. Jardine. This one is for Mr. Sakumoto."

The old man stopped by Luana's bench, watching while she attached another piece of string to her needle with nimble fingers, and began the process of pushing the blossoms on. One to the right, one to the left. When finished, the lei was a beautiful flattened circle, frilled at the edges, while appearing braided at the center.

"I'll be there at the anniversary party. Along with all of Malino, I expect. You'll be there, won't you, Luana?"

Luana nodded. "Couldn't keep me away."

As he said, the entire town would be there to wish the Sakumotos well on their fiftieth anniversary. It would be a great party; Luana just wished she could get up more enthusiasm for it. She almost didn't hear Mr. Jardine's last few words, saying that he'd see her, along with her beautiful leis, later.

As she pushed another vanda onto her needle, Luana watched Mr. Jardine move away down the street. But instead of the bright Aloha shirt and the khaki slacks, she saw a blue polo shirt and faded jeans. The baseball cap became a head of light brown hair, streaked with blond highlights. And the figure filling the clothes did not belong to her familiar neighbor. Instead of a slow-moving, elderly man, she saw one who was younger, more muscular, one who moved with quick confidence and with a sense of accomplishing things.

Luana stared. Then she blinked, keeping her eyes closed for a full five seconds. When she opened them, Mr. Jardine in his Aloha shirt once again strolled slowly down the sidewalk, waving a greeting to someone inside the restaurant. Probably Mele, getting the tables set for dinner.

Jake was invading her private space a lot these days. Too much. Luana hoped spending more time with him, introducing him to some Island musical acts, would work to dispel the images filling her mind and her dreams. That was the mature way to deal with infatuation, wasn't it? And this had to be nothing more than infatuation. Luana didn't even want to consider what she would do if it wasn't.

What were the options if her plan backfired and spending more time with him just made her like him more? He couldn't take up any more of her time, could he? There were only twenty-four hours in a day, after all, and he was already on her mind for at least half of that. Maybe more. Probably more, since he'd started invading her night time dreams as well.

With a sigh, Luana resolutely turned her mind to that

nice young couple from Seattle and their Christmas wedding. Unlike Jake, they were interested in a garden wedding. There was a portion of the garden where a tall hedge of poinsettias should be brilliantly blooming by Christmas. She'd have to remember to tell them about it.

Jake's thoughts too were filled with Luana. While he ate a lonely dinner at the Terrace Restaurant, Luana's face and figure flooded his mind. Again and again, he saw her lovely face, her tempting lips. Her swaying hips.

He finally pushed away his half-eaten meal. Even the beautiful music didn't help to distract him from memories of Luana. After all, she was responsible for his being here; she had recommended the entertainers who performed during the dinner hour. There were other restaurants in the resort, several with reputations for innovative cuisine. Without her endorsement, he might well have chosen one of those. But he'd come to hear the music. Nostalgia over their pleasant luncheon together there had nothing to do with his choice.

Of course not. He was a businessman, well respected in his field. He had his choice of sophisticated women to date on the mainland. Unfortunately, he wasn't on the mainland at the moment. And he wouldn't be for a while.

Still, a local girl from the country—by her own admission—was not the kind of person he should be dreaming about. He was young. Just because his much younger half-sister wanted to get married was no reason to feel that he should be taking the big step himself. No reason to look at every woman he found appealing as a potential date.

He'd no sooner reassured himself on this point than a concerned waitress was fluttering at his side, removing the discarded plate, still half full.

"Was there a problem with your meal, sir?"

The young woman was very pretty, flirting with him in as obvious a manner as she could without getting into trouble with the management. But Jake couldn't summon up any interest in her.

He managed a cheerful smile. "The food is excellent. I'm just not very hungry this evening."

He spent a few minutes bantering with her, but his heart wasn't in it. The waitress's blond good looks seemed out of place in the tropics, her blue eyes washed out. His mind continued to return to Luana, to the lush beauty of her wild dark hair, to the life sparkling in her deep brown eyes. And to his parting words to her earlier that day. *"It's a date."*

Of course, it wouldn't be a date in the traditional sense. It would not be dinner and a movie, or a concert followed by drinks or dessert. But the two of them would be going out together, even if just to church. It could count as a date in his book.

Then Jake had a startling thought. Would she bring anyone with her? A friend? A relative? Her *mother*? Church attendance usually involved families. While she said she would be taking him to hear the music, that didn't mean that it wasn't her family church and that she would not have the entire family in the car with her. He wasn't ready to meet her family!

Jake frowned so mightily, he frightened his waitress who had just returned with the dessert menu. He ordered a dessert he didn't want to make up for it, and added a large tip to his bill when he signed the receipt.

He continued to nibble at the chocolate macadamia nut pie as he enjoyed the floor show and drank most of a pot of coffee. The music was great and he didn't think he'd be doing a lot of sleeping that night anyway. Not as long as a certain pretty face insisted on troubling his thoughts. Nibbling on forkfuls of chocolate pie might be nice, but nibbling on Luana's ears and lips would be infinitely more satisfying.

Shaking his head clear of that image, Jake forced himself to wonder what she was doing on this balmy Friday evening. Was she at home with her family, perhaps listening to music and thinking of him?

Who was he trying to kid? For an attractive young woman like Luana, it was undoubtedly date night.

His eyes rested on a young couple at the table across from his. They had been lingering over coffee as he was, their chairs inching closer together as the evening progressed. Probably a local couple out on a date. Getting to know each other. He noticed they were holding hands.

Could Luana be out on a date now, holding hands with some local guy like the one opposite? Jake checked him out. He was nicely dressed in a conservative Hawaiian shirt and dress pants. He'd already learned that passed for dress-up clothes in Hawaii. He supposed a woman would think the man handsome—if she liked a guy with thick wavy hair, a deep tan, and a mustache. His date was laughing up at him and he flashed her a smile that showed off a deep dimple.

Jake signaled the waitress and ordered a drink.

It didn't take long for his mind to wander back to its favorite subject these days. Luana Young.

The previous day's luncheon had been one of the most enjoyable he'd had in a long time. People had been telling him he worked too hard, combining lunches and dinners with business meetings. But it was what he'd done yesterday too, and look what had happened this time.

Luana was a great companion. She could speak knowledgeably about music, books, and movies, all things he liked to talk about. While sincere in her opinions, she didn't try to force them on him, respecting his right to form his own. She'd even determined to listen again to an artist she'd once dismissed, because of Jake's arguments over the man's musical genius.

And she wasn't afraid to laugh at herself, telling him about embarrassing childhood moments in ways that made them both laugh. Jake could have listened to her all afternoon.

A flash of guilt hit him as he realized that he'd steered the conversation over to her again and again. He'd learned a lot about her and what she liked, and about the small town where she'd grown up. But he had told her virtually nothing about himself.

Jake placated himself with the knowledge that it was a necessary evil, and that he would tell her everything as soon as Callie arrived. He *had* let drop the fact that he lived in California. True, it was a small thing, but more than she'd known yesterday.

And for now he had their date on Sunday to look forward to. Forget the invisible quotation marks he'd been putting around the word in his mind. It was a morning date and he'd make the best of the day, whether it involved just the two of them or her entire family.

On his way out of the restaurant, he stopped to speak to the hostess. It had occurred to him that he might draw out their time together on Sunday morning by suggesting brunch afterward. He had to find out the best places, and flirting with the pretty Japanese-American hostess took his mind off Luana for a few minutes.

* * *

As Jake bantered with the hostess at the Kukui Wana'ao Resort, Luana stood before the mirror in her bedroom in Malino, brushing out her hair and thinking about Sunday. Thankfully, she had a full day planned for Saturday. She was spending the day with her old *halau*, helping the hula troupe make leis and skirts for their upcoming Aloha Week performances. She had promised that she would keep some of the things in her large refrigerator at the store, so that they could do them all at once. School had already started and many of the members were busy with other activities. Luana had been looking forward to the get-together, now more so than ever. She'd be too busy to think about Jake.

Luana put down the brush and climbed into bed. She pulled the sheet over her and sighed. Thinking of Jake just before retiring was not going to help her go to sleep.

Thoughts of the upcoming Sunday played through her mind. However the day went, she'd have to see him again next week; besides her promise to introduce him to Island music, she had promised to teach him origami.

I wonder if he'll be good at that, she thought, her lips softening into a dreamy smile. *Or clumsy.*

An instant picture of his long fingers came into view, waving a sweet roll under her nose, holding up little jars of jam and honey. They were tanned fingers, competent-looking. Long and narrow, too, like those of an artist, or a pianist. She saw those fingers reaching toward her, thought of them touching her cheek in a gentle caress.

The smile left her lips, and she had to run the tip of her tongue over them. Suddenly, her mouth and lips were very dry; her hands tightened on the sheet, pulling the fabric tight against her toes.

Once again she wondered what he did. In California. It was one more piece of the puzzle she had, one little thing to add to the tidbits she knew about his life: he had long fingers and well-tended nails, a modish hair style, and fashionable clothes. And he lived in California.

It wasn't much.

Luana frowned into the dark. How could she allow a man who wouldn't even tell her what he did for a living to invade her life this way? She had to get a grip on herself.

With these words, and a simmering anger, Luana slipped into a restless slumber.

Chapter Seven

Jake was ready before their agreed time of 8:30 on Sunday, standing outside the main entrance of the Kukui Wana'ao Resort. He expected Luana to arrive promptly. She had been punctual in all their dealings so far, a trait he found admirable; perhaps partly because he tended to be on time himself, while Callie never was. Getting that girl to adhere to a schedule was like pulling teeth from a grizzly bear. He didn't envy her road manager his job, that was for sure. The man reminded him of a Marine; it was one of the main reasons he'd hired him. The position needed someone who could take charge, and who would not be intimidated by a pint-sized superstar.

Shaking thoughts of his sister from his head, Jake smiled a greeting to the car runners. So early on a Sunday morning, several of them were standing near the entrance with little to do. Jake began to visit, learning that one of the young men played in a band that entertained at the resort two nights a week.

Although involved in his conversation, Jake still managed to keep watch for Luana. He didn't know what kind of car she drove, but he knew he'd recognize her.

And he did.

His new friend was complaining about the competitive local entertainment market, because of the numerous young bands available, when Jake spotted the yellow Volkswagen. One of the old-style Beetles, it was clean and appeared newly waxed. For Jake, there was no mistaking the profile behind the wheel. The long swan's neck, held in a regal manner, the dark hair pulled back but leaving a halo of wispy curls framing her face.

And all alone in the car.

Jake grinned.

"Oh, you waiting for Luana?"

Jake had almost forgotten that he was conversing with the young car runner. He turned back toward him, reluctantly removing his gaze from the driver of the approaching car.

"Yes. She's taking me to a local church to hear the music."

The Volkswagen came to a stop and his companion opened the passenger side door.

"Enjoy yourself, eh."

He waved a friendly good-bye to the couple as Luana pulled around the circular drive.

"Good morning."

Luana wondered if Jake would notice the hesitation in her voice. She'd been looking forward to this moment for the past two days, but now that it was here she felt flustered.

"You look terrific."

Luana was stopped at the resort entrance road, waiting to turn onto the Queen Ka'ahumanu Highway. So she chanced a look over to Jake as she murmured her thanks.

Jake was smiling at her, his eyes glowing with admiration. Something electric flew between them as their eyes met, hitting Luana near her heart. Her lips formed a smile without consulting her, but the fluttering beneath her breastbone raised alarm bells.

She resolutely turned her attention back to the road, hoping her voice would remain steady when she spoke.

"I guess this is the first time you've seen me in anything other than the official resort muumuu."

She'd donned a red muumuu this morning, her favorite one. She wore her strappy, heeled sandals with it, but she doubted he could see them while she was driving. She'd put her hair up, too, and pinned two gardenias into the dark mass of curls.

"You look good in red."

The sincerity in his voice made Luana's cheeks turn pink as she once again murmured her thanks. She wasn't trying to attract him. She reminded herself that she hadn't dressed up just for him; she always dressed up for church.

While Jake refrained from speaking for a few minutes, Luana strained to see what she could of him through her peripheral vision. His head was turned. He was probably enjoying the scenery.

Luana scolded herself for thinking she could get to know this man, then let him return to the mainland without getting hurt.

Jake's voice startled her out of her distressing thoughts.

"Great car."

"Thanks. My brother calls it a banana, but I call her Betty."

"Kind of like Beetle. I like it."

Luana broke into a wide grin. "That's it. That's exactly why I named her Betty. Betty Beetle. Most people don't get it."

"How long have you had her?"

Luana liked the way he referred to the car as "her." She referred to it that way herself, but all her brothers made fun of her.

"Since college. I inherited her from my older brother."

"So you have siblings."

It was a comment, but Luana took it as an inquiry and began to tell him about her family. Although Jake had planned to enjoy the scenery on their ride, he found himself watching her animated features instead. And drinking in the delicious scent of the gardenias she wore in her hair.

"I have three brothers and a sister. They're all older except for one brother, Kimo. He's a musician. He plays the guitar at the church we're going to."

She rattled on about some of the people at the church, but Jake barely heard her. He loved the sound of her voice. He could have happily spent the rest of the day in her small car, cramped as it was. The titillating scent of the gardenias, mixed with the briny sea air, was more intoxicating than any alcoholic libation.

It seemed like seconds, but was about fifteen minutes later when Luana pulled into the church lot. Jake didn't know what he'd expected, but he was surprised by the small church.

"Wow."

Luana set the parking brake and smiled. "You like it?"

Picturesque was an understatement. The tiny church would have been at home in any New England village. Nestled among coconut palms and *hala* trees, the church was a dollhouse of a building with white painted sides and a blue corrugated tin roof. There was a traditional steeple on the near end of the roof, and arched windows lined the side, with hydrangeas blooming below.

Set against the beauty of the mist-shrouded Kohala mountains, there was a mysterious, otherworldly look to the old church. Making the whole picture calendar-perfect, there was a rainbow arcing from the clouds over the mountains to the green pastures that stretched out behind the church.

On a wide porch at the front, a man in liturgical robes greeted the arriving congregation. The minister, Jake presumed.

Jake was not a regular churchgoer. As a child, his mother took him every Sunday. His father was usually busy at work, even on the Lord's Day. So once his mother died, Jake did not visit church much. However, he did enjoy services when he made the effort to attend, and he especially loved the music. Whenever he was in Europe, he made it a priority to visit the great cathedrals, not only for the classic and beautiful architecture, but for the music played and sung there. Jake loved music, music of all kinds.

This small-town church, though, with its friendly congregants hugging one another in greeting, was one that Jake could easily envision himself joining.

"It looks like a movie setting for a romantic wedding."

Jake immediately regretted his choice of words.

Luana leaped forward with the expected question.

"You wouldn't want to move the ceremony here?" Luana's eyebrows raised along with her voice as she asked the question. "It's called *Aloha Ke Akua,* 'Love of God'," she translated.

"No." His reply was quick. Callie would love the church, but there was no question of using it. The entire area was too open, with acres of mountains behind it, a long stretch of beach across from it; both were prime locations for hiding photographers with telephoto lenses. "But it is a beautiful church. It looks old."

"It is. Dates back to the monarchy, but a lot of it has been rebuilt. There was a problem with termites."

Luana led him to the door, where she introduced Jake to a member of the congregation who gave him a warm welcome and a shell lei.

Inside, it was small but cozy. The building was positioned so that the sea breeze blew through the windows from *makai* to *mauka,* providing a comfortable coolness even without air-conditioning. The narrow arched windows which lined both sides of the oblong room were filled with stained glass in varying shades of blue. As the bright sunlight filtered through these windows, it created an illusion of being under the sea. At the front of the room a small koa altar had pride of place; beside it, an equally beautiful koa podium.

A quilt hung behind the altar, a large quilt in green and white with the leafy green design all cut from one giant piece of cloth. Jake had seen many quilts over the years, but never anything like this. It was beautiful, and he could imagine the admiration among his upscale friends in San Francisco if they saw this. Not a series of patches or an "art" quilt, the beauty of the design and the simplicity of color would add to any room.

Luana must have seen his interest in the quilt. She leaned

toward him to explain that it was a traditional Hawaiian quilt in the *ulu* pattern.

"You might have heard it called breadfruit," she told him. "It was the staple of the ancient Hawaiian diet—the bread of life, you might say."

Making it totally appropriate to hang in a Hawaiian church, Jake thought.

Jake enjoyed the service, which included Hawaiian hymns sung joyfully by the entire congregation. They were led by a small choir which included several musicians. Guitar, ukulele, drums, and keyboard were more than enough to underscore the lovely hymns.

Afterward, Luana introduced him to the members of the choir and band. Luana was impressed with the way Jake interacted with the local musicians. He seemed to know just what to say and what questions to ask. She could see that the small group was flattered by his interest, especially as he seemed so knowledgeable about music and music production. Once again she wondered what he did for a living. Could he have something to do with the music industry? A music producer, perhaps? Wouldn't that be a wonderful thing for her musician friends.

Luana was pulled from her speculation by a noisy invitation.

"A bunch of us are going to Hilo next Sunday after church for the slack key guitar festival," her brother Kimo said.

"Hey, yeah," another member said. "If you still here, maybe you like come?"

If Jake was surprised by the invitation, he didn't show it. He seemed interested, even as he raised his left brow and looked over to Luana.

"Slack key guitar, you say?"

Before Luana could answer, the previous speaker did.

"Yeah. It's *da kine* Hawaiian-style guitar playing, you know? Kind of like country, but all our own."

Jake nodded. "Sounds good. And I will be here. If you don't mind having me, I'd love to come." Once again he looked toward Luana. "If it's all right with Luana, that is?" His voice moved upward at the end of the sentence, forming it into a question.

Luana blushed, her cheeks turning an attractive pink even as she frowned. Really, the man was making it sound as if they had a serious relationship between them. Asking her permission that way! And in front of her brother! She could see the question in Kimo's eye. He'd be interrogating her about this before the week was out!

But she could also see the enthusiasm Jake felt for the music. It was apparent in his appreciation of the Sunday service, and in the potential of the festival the men mentioned.

"By all means, Jake, you should go. Slack key guitar music is wonderful." She frowned at him. "But I have no idea why I have to give my permission."

Jake started to say something, apparently thought better of it, and turned to his new friends.

"Next Sunday then?" He extended his hand to shake on it.

"We leave right after church. Couple guys got vans, so we don't all have to drive."

"The festival runs all day," Kimo told Jake. "People come and go. We make one day of it."

"Yeah," the man on his right added. "On the way, we stop at Tex's in Honokaa for *malassadas*. In Hilo, we'll have some lunch. Maybe dinner."

"Tex's Drive-in is famous for their *malassadas*," Luana informed him.

"*Malassadas?*"

Jake was beginning to look like he was out of his league. Luana had to smile. It was tough to take large doses of someone with such enormous confidence—not that it was any help in making him less appealing. But she'd like to see another side of him.

"You don't know *malassadas?*" Jake received a hearty slap on the back from Kimo. "Man, you gotta come then. You need to try them."

Luana smiled at Jake. She'd save him.

"*Malassadas* are Portuguese fried donuts. They don't have a hole, and they're rolled in sugar."

"Ah." Jake nodded. "I've had the Portuguese sweet rolls. Very good."

Jake turned to Luana. "The guitar festival sounds like a great way to spend the day. You'll be going too, won't you?"

Luana hesitated. It did sound like fun. And her new strategy was supposed to be spending as much time as possible with him. But she didn't want to be the only woman going either.

"Is it only the guys going?"

Jake smiled at her. It sounded to him like she wanted to go, but didn't want to interfere if it was a guy bonding thing. Happily, one of his newfound friends answered her unspoken question.

"Oh, no. My wife is coming. And Henry's girlfriend."

They spent a few minutes more talking about the trip, before exchanging friendly good-byes, and heading for the parking lot. As they walked toward Betty, Jake invited Luana to have brunch with him.

"I can't, Jake. Really," she added as she saw that he was ready to press the point. "I promised that I would go to see my old hula troupe perform in Kona today. It's the beginning of the Aloha Festivals, and they're part of a program with some other prestigious schools. It was an honor that they were invited. In fact I spent most of yesterday with them helping make ti leaf skirts and leis."

Jake's interest was piqued. His eyes sparkled.

"Can I go with you? I'd love to see them perform."

Luana didn't really want any more togetherness with Jake, but how could she refuse when he was so enthused, so anxious to learn more? And it was such a good chance to teach him more about Hawaiian culture. That opportunity was too difficult for her to resist. Thoughts of her new strategy were more than enough to tip the balance.

"Okay. I'll take you."

"Let's stop for brunch on the way. I understand the brunch at the Kukui Wana'ao is extraordinary."

Luana was surprised at his excellent pronunciation. Most tourists could barely get their tongues around the resort name, but he said it perfectly. He even remembered that the W was pronounced like a V. Once again she was impressed by him.

Luana sighed. She *wanted* to spend more time with him, which made her think it was a bad idea. He was too handsome, too charming. Too appealing.

She knew nothing about him, and he lived thousands of miles away.

Luana realized that he was watching her carefully as she tried to make a decision. His eyes, the same color as the ocean across the road, pleaded with her. And she did have the resort management's exhortation to treat him with her best Aloha spirit.

"Okay. But we can stop anywhere. I don't want you to spend that much money on brunch."

"It's not a problem. Besides, I heard all about it from the hostess at the restaurant the other night, and I want to experience it myself. You wouldn't want to deprive me of that, would you?"

He looked so woeful, Luana had to laugh. So of course she agreed to brunch at the Kukui Wana'ao. And added actor to her mental list of his possible occupations.

"Since we're going to stop at the resort anyway, why don't you let me drive into Kona? You can be navigator."

Luana was ready to object, but as often happened, he seemed to anticipate what she was going to say.

"I love to drive," he assured her. "And I have a great rental car."

Jake's great car was a Mercedes convertible. Luana shouldn't have been surprised. After all, he was a valued guest at the Kukui Wana'ao. That alone presupposed money, and lots of it.

But the thought of arriving in Kona—where her friends might see her—in the nifty silver car, had her once again proposing to drive Betty instead.

"No offense to Betty, Luana, but my legs are longer than her front end." Jake waved aside the hotel valet and ushered her to the car himself, opening the passenger side door and helping her in. "You'll love riding with the top down."

It was Luana's first experience of a convertible. They weren't the most practical of cars in the Kohala area, where misty rain was a frequent, almost daily, companion. But Luana could now understand why they were so popular. On a sunny day like this one, it was a heady feeling riding along in the stylish car. The sun was warm on her head and shoulders, the breeze cooling. The smell of the sea air was pervasive and invigorating; by the time they arrived in Kona she was already hungry again. And after all she'd eaten at the extravagant Kukui Wana'ao buffet!

Brunch with Jake had been wonderful. It was like a rerun of their luncheon on Thursday. Conversation flowed, smiles and laughter were plentiful, and something electric filled the air between them—something she didn't want to explore too closely. At least not yet.

Perhaps that was another reason the open car had been so enjoyable, Luana thought, as she busied herself trying to fix her windblown hair while Jake put the top of the car up. All that fast-moving air helped neutralize the energy field that seemed to coexist with them.

Jake finally opened her door, offering his hand. An invitation she could not resist. As her fingers closed around his, the familiar tingle raced up her arm. What was it about this man? It was as though he had an electrical field around him, a strange kind of energy-packed aura. And every time she crossed it, something zapped her heart.

"There's an ice cream shop," Jake said, his voice carrying the excitement of a seven-year-old boy. "I could go for a cone. Don't you find the sea air invigorating?"

Luana smiled, once again struck by the way their minds seemed to work in sync.

"If there's time before your show, of course," Jake added.

In her confusion over her reaction to Jake, Luana had almost forgotten the reason for the trip to Kona. Reminded, she glanced at her watch. "There's time."

She melted as easily as ice cream in the warm afternoon sun when Jake flashed a delighted grin.

"Then let's go."

Chapter Eight

The afternoon passed quickly. Both of them lost themselves in the beauty of the musical numbers. Even introducing Jake to all her old friends was okay. The winks and *shakas* she received behind his back showed that he'd made a good impression.

Don't get complacent, Luana, she told herself, as they returned to the car under a starry sky. Jake had taken her hand, and he swung it gently as they walked back to the parking lot.

"The stars are so beautiful here," Jake said. "I never notice them much in the city."

"Too much light," Luana told him. She let her gaze move upward. Thousands of stars glittered in the black sky. "They look even better in Malino."

"Really? Your hometown, right?"

Luana merely nodded, forgetting that it was dark, that

they were walking, that he was probably looking ahead or upward at the skies.

"I'd like to see it sometime."

The thought startled Luana, and she tripped on a rough spot on the sidewalk. Jake immediately reached out to support her. Warmth rushed through her, welcome in the cool night air, and she was tempted to hang onto him. Instead, she merely thanked him, then pulled back to her original place beside him.

But they were already at their destination. Jake squeezed her hand before releasing it and guiding her up the two steps that led into the parking lot.

Luana approached the passenger side door and stood waiting to be let inside. Jake removed the keys from his pocket but made no effort to unlock the door. He was standing very close, looking down into Luana's upturned face. When he spoke, his voice was thick with feeling.

"It's hard to believe anything could be more beautiful."

Mesmerized by his voice, Luana returned his stare. Her voice too was huskier than usual. "The stars?"

"I can see the stars in your eyes."

Did he mean the stars were beautiful, or her eyes? Did her dark eyes reflect the nighttime sky? His were as blue as always. She couldn't see any stars in them, but she could detect admiration and something else that might be desire.

Luana blinked, breaking the spell. What was she thinking? She glanced down at her sandaled feet, anywhere but back into his luscious eyes. She forced a laugh.

"There aren't any stars in my eyes, Jake. It's much too bright in the parking lot. You city boys are just full of flattery."

She could see Jake's surprise. He was wondering what

had happened to the romantic mood he'd created by holding her hand and admiring the stars.

And their walk had been romantic. He could charm with words and actions as well as looks and she would have to be on her guard. She refused to be a tourist's vacation fantasy. Some of the local girls didn't mind dating a handsome tourist for a week or two. Especially if he had money and could show her a good time. But Luana wasn't like that. If she dated Jake for the next four weeks and fell for him, she would be devastated when he left. And with his looks and charm, that's exactly what would happen. That's why she had to break the romantic mood. She had seen where it was going, and a kiss beside the car had been the next logical step.

Luana stifled a sigh of regret as she settled into the car. Jake was a fun guy to be with, no doubt about that. But there were still too many problems, not the least of which was his continuing silence about his personal life. She'd keep the integrity of her convictions and see that their relationship was strictly a friendship. But how easy it would be to forget and live in the moment.

During the next week, Luana and Jake spent all their afternoons and evenings together. Aloha Festival events were scattered over several weeks, the shows and celebrations staggered among the various islands and cities. Jake enjoyed the Big Island programs, loved the music and the shows. He took such pleasure from it, Luana spent all her spare time planning more excursions. His enjoyment brought her happiness too. And he was behaving himself, as there had been no more romantic interludes. Luana just wasn't sure if she was happy or disappointed about that!

Jake also loved driving around the island. Between his

morning swims and the open car, he was acquiring a beautiful golden tan that made him more attractive than ever. Luana noted the looks he drew as they drove through towns and entered stadiums and parks for concerts.

Jake also had a brand-new digital camera, and would take numerous photos of scenery and events. He asked questions about the Islands and local customs, commented on what he saw and learned, would sometimes pull off the highway so he could get out to view something he considered special.

Luana recalled how concerned she was the first time this happened. They were driving to Hilo to view a special hula *halau* presentation on the life of Kamehameha the Great, tooling along the Hamakua coast in Jake's rental car. Luana had quickly become a fan of convertibles. The sun was shining, the top was down, the ride was smooth. And the company was top-notch.

As Luana began to contemplate her burgeoning friendship with Jake, the object of her daydreams suddenly pulled the car over onto the shoulder and cut the engine.

Luana came instantly to attention.

"What's wrong? Is it a flat tire?" She hadn't felt anything, but the pulling of a flat was most noticeable to the person driving.

But Jake's excited expression belied any serious problem.

"Nothing's wrong. Don't worry." He reached over and patted her hand with his, then continued leaning across her to take his camera from the glove box. "There's no problem. I just wanted to check out that waterfall. Didn't you see it?"

A waterfall? How could he expect her to think about a waterfall when he was sitting there distracting her?

Jake stepped out of the car. Luana, however, was still trying to get over the blizzard of sensations that had showered over her when he leaned across her. His upper arm had brushed her chest, his elbow pushed into her thigh as he opened the glove compartment and reached inside for the camera. The sensation of heat and the minor shivers she'd felt at previous contacts were nothing compared to what happened with these brief touches. An avalanche of feeling pounded her, making her uncertain she could stand if she tried to leave the car.

Luana swallowed. How could he be thinking of taking pictures when she was such an emotional wreck? Didn't he feel anything at all?

Luana reached up to try and control her flyaway hair, twisting her neck at the same time, trying to see back along the road they had just traversed.

"I wasn't really paying attention. There are quite a few small waterfalls along this road. There are a couple of large ones too, but much further along."

"Small ones? Really? And you say there are big ones too?"

Jake was as enthused as a young child. Luana had to smile as she pushed her hair back behind her ears. The more time she spent with him, the more she found that his charm was a natural component of his personality. To know him was to like him. Although Mele insisted on teasing her about Jake and her feelings for him, Luana refused to think beyond liking. Theirs was a pleasant friendship, a *short* pleasant friendship. After all, Jake would be leaving right after the wedding. She would do well to keep reminding herself of that indisputable fact.

"Aren't you coming?"

Jake stood outside her door, his body almost quivering

with suppressed energy; it was obvious he was anxious to backtrack along the road and view the waterfall. Luana stepped out. As soon as her feet hit the dusty shoulder, Jake took her arm, steering her back the way they'd come.

As always when he touched her, Luana could feel heat. She'd stopped thinking it strange and just accepted it as the way it was between them. From his fingers near her elbow, warmth radiated up her arm and across her shoulders. From there it traveled up her neck and down through her mid-section. If he held her long enough, the heat traveled all the way to her toes. It had nothing to do with the atmospheric temperature. It happened on cool evenings when he escorted her from a late concert. It happened on sweltering afternoons, when they sat on tatami mats with bento lunches.

And it was happening now, on a warm but humid afternoon with the comfortably cool trade winds blowing across her too-warm body.

Luana kept to the extreme edge of the shoulder while Jake steered her toward a clump of trees. Long grass tickled her ankles as they approached the thick grouping of guava, *hau,* and African tulip trees that almost hid a small rocky stream. Clear mountain water flowed rapidly toward them. Some hundred feet *mauka,* the stream bed dropped, creating the waterfall that had precipitated their stop.

Jake halted, grinning at the sight.

"Look at that! Doesn't it make you want to take off your shoes and go wading?"

Luana raised her eyebrows.

"Are you kidding? Look at those rocks in the stream bed. And that water comes straight off the mountain." Her shoulders shook in a minor shiver. "It's probably freezing."

Jake clicked his tongue, shooting her an indulgent look.

"Luana. You need to relax. Play a little. You work too hard."

His eyes turned toward the stream and trees, then back to Luana. Cars continued to speed by on Route 19, making Luana nervous about their proximity to the highway. But Jake didn't seem to notice.

"I'm a hard worker, too, Luana. Like you. In fact, I've been working hard for the last two years. Never bothered with a vacation. Rarely took time off. Didn't have time. Don't get me wrong, I really like my work, so it's not a hardship." He gazed thoughtfully at the beauty of the scene before him. "I think one of the reasons Callie maneuvered me into arranging her wedding was to force me into taking a vacation. She figured while I was here, waiting around for everything to be settled, I could rest on the beach, catch up on my reading. A forced vacation." He laughed, flashing a sardonic smile toward Luana. "I always think I'm taking care of her, but I guess it works both ways."

"You look after each other." Luana nodded. "It's what family members do."

Jake grinned at her. "Yeah. I guess it is."

He raised the camera, and got ready to take a few shots while Luana noted that he did not refute her statement that Callie was family. Another tiny piece of the puzzle.

"Callie gave me this camera, too. Told me I needed a hobby."

Luana smiled. "I'd say she was right. You seem pretty enthusiastic about taking pictures." She rolled her eyes. "No wonder you wanted to leave at three o'clock for a seven-o'clock concert."

Jake ignored her sardonic tone and checked the camera, pulling Luana close to show her his shots and help chose the ones to save. Once again, she was overcome by the radiant heat of his body. How could the man function? He never looked hot, either, but appeared cool and comfortable whatever the situation.

Finally, he stepped aside and put the camera in his pocket. He placed his arm around her waist and began the short trek back to the car. Luana felt the familiar warmth begin again. The strange phenomenon was beginning to impart a feeling of comfort. As was the way he guided her along the side of the busy highway, making her feel safe from the speeding traffic.

"It wasn't always that way between Callie and me." Jake spoke casually, returning to their earlier topic. "There's such a big age difference, it made it hard for us to get to know each other. And feel comfortable together."

Luana remained silent as they approached the car, afraid to break the spell. Jake was revealing a lot about himself with these small confidences. She would bet Callie was his sister. A much younger sister.

Jake led her to the car, opening and holding the door for her. Part of his charm was his beautiful manners, a trait that could be called old-fashioned in the twenty-first century. Yet polite tendencies like these were not to be dismissed, but savored; they made a woman feel treasured and special.

Jake hurried around the car, got in and pulled back onto the road.

"It's a great day, isn't it? Nice weather, nice scenery, nice company."

Luana released the breath she hardly realized she'd been holding. It seemed he was done sharing aspects of his personal life. Instead he threw her a flirtatious smile and turned completely away from any implications she might have made from his recent words. He began to comment on the island's topography and the highway itself, and the problems it must have caused when they endeavored to build it.

"A lot of the work was done during the thirties, through President Roosevelt's programs. Those old stone bridges for instance. I remember my grandparents talking about it."

"Amazing." Jake was driving attentively, but still trying to take in all the sights. "The housing styles are very interesting too. It's not like anything I've seen before."

Luana smiled looking about her. They were passing through one of the old small towns or "camps."

"These are old plantation houses. It was all sugar cane fields out here for years and years. Even when I was young, there was still a lot of cane out this way. But all the plantations are gone now."

"What do you mean by plantation houses?"

As Luana went on to explain about the homes made available for the workers on the plantation, Jake listened attentively. Once again, Luana was impressed with his sincere interest in her island's history and lifestyle.

And he was really enjoying the Hawaiian music. No one could fake the way he watched and listened with rapt attention at all of the events they attended. Afterward, if at all possible, he spoke to the performers about their work and their vision.

On their Sunday excursion with the group from the church, Jake spent more time inside the auditorium listening to the slack key guitar performances than any of the other members of their group. While the others ran out for lunch, he stayed to listen. Luana didn't know if he even remembered she was there, until he took her hand during one especially moving piece.

Her brother pulled her aside at one point to comment on

Jake's interest, and to question her about her relationship with him. She'd reacted badly, she remembered, telling him to mind his own business and calling him "little brother." She wondered how long it would be before he had a talk with their parents, and her mother came to her room for a girl-to-woman talk. Sometimes her parents forgot she was several years beyond twenty-one and treated her like a teenager again.

Luana was remembering their day on the following Monday as she waited for Jake to arrive for his first origami lesson. For his only origami lesson, she corrected herself. There was no reason for it to extend beyond this one lesson. After today, she wouldn't have to spend so much time in his company. The wedding plans were well in hand, the Aloha Festival activities winding down, and she could go back to her regular routine. Jake could go back to vacationing—sunbathing on the beach or taking pictures where he pleased.

Jake arrived bearing gifts—his usual breakfast treat of rolls and coffee—and a manila envelope.

"I thought I'd better bring food," he said, setting the tray on an empty corner of her desk. He set the manila envelope on his usual chair. "I'll bet you're not eating breakfast anymore, now that we aren't meeting first thing in the morning."

Luana didn't answer. She'd only have to confirm what he said.

"Ah-ha. I knew it." He handed her a cup of coffee, already prepared the way she liked it, and offered her the basket.

Luana had to smile. *"Malassadas?"* She reached into the basket and took one, even though she knew it would leave a sugary mess on her hands and she would have to go and wash them before the lesson. "You must have really liked them, huh?"

"I decided your friends were correct. The *malassadas* at Tex's Drive-in are without doubt superior. These, however, are darn good."

Luana had to agree. "They are. But I'm going to be a blimp if you don't stop bringing me all this fattening food in the morning."

Jake waved away her fears. "You have a long way to go before you can even approach blimp status." He offered the basket again. "Here, have another."

Luana laughed and took another. They visited while they finished the snack, then headed off to wash up before beginning the origami lesson. With all their excursions the week before, there hadn't been time to fit it in, and now there were just two weeks left before the wedding.

But Jake had a surprise for her before they began. Returning to her office, he picked up the manila envelope and presented it to her with a flourish.

"I thought you might enjoy having these, Luana. A little remembrance of your Aloha Festival."

With a quizzical smile and a soft thank-you, Luana accepted the envelope and looked inside. Large glossy photographs fell onto her desk as she tipped the envelope. The photos covered most of the events they had enjoyed the previous week, with the majority of them her friends at her old *halau*. As she spread them out for a better look, tears filled her eyes.

"I wasn't able to include any from the weekend, but I thought you'd like to have these of your friends."

Luana listened to his gentle voice and wished he wasn't such a nice man. How could she keep him at a distance when he insisted on doing such special things?

"Thank you." She blinked rapidly, wishing the tears to perdition. "They're wonderful. You have a real talent for photography."

Jake waved away her praise. But he reached forward, placing his fingers on her chin and tipping her face upward.

"I didn't mean to make you cry. Just offer a little thank-you of my own for giving up your time and showing me around the way you did."

Luana smiled, blinking a few more times, unsuccessfully. "They're happy tears," she assured him. "*Mahalo,* Jake."

She reached up to wipe away a tear that had gotten away and started to roll down her cheek. But Jake got to it first. His long fingers, tanned now to a deep gold, brushed lightly across her cheek, erasing the lone droplet. He was very close, too close, Luana thought. Would he lean forward a little more, until their lips touched?

Luana wanted it so much, she was disappointed when all he did was murmur "You're welcome" in a soft, husky voice. His hands returned to his side, and he stepped back.

"I especially liked these," he said, separating out several of the pictures.

Luana nodded blindly, still shocked at how much she'd wanted his kiss. She took her seat, trying to return to some semblance of normalcy. They spent a few minutes looking at the photos and reminiscing about the events. Then Luana shuffled them back into the envelope and pulled out the gold origami paper.

Luana had barely begun to show him how to make the folds when she knew this lesson was going to be a trial. She couldn't tell if he was being contrary or if he really did have trouble making the folds. But she had to get much too close in order to direct his hands. The intensity of their earlier moments over the photographs made it even more difficult. She suspected he was enjoying every minute.

And he was.

"This way?"

Jake purposely folded the bit of gold paper in the wrong direction. He loved the way Luana scolded him gently, then held his fingers to direct him in the proper step. Her head bent over his hands as she concentrated on the moves, and he took deep breaths of her marvelous scent. There were no gardenias in her hair today, so it wasn't the intoxicating and exotic spice of that flower that filled his nostrils. The gardenias had driven him wild on that first Sunday morning, filling the little Volkswagen with their special perfume. It was another reason he'd insisted on driving the convertible. Safer by far.

Today, Luana smelled of something far more subtle. It didn't seem to be perfume or cologne. His guess was that she used a flower-scented soap. Perhaps jasmine, as he continued to associate that particular flower with her. Or it might be her shampoo. With her head bent over their hands, her hair was tickling his nostrils. He hoped he wouldn't sneeze, but otherwise the sensation was a pleasant one. Much more pleasant than their earlier brush over the photographs. That had been sheer agony. He'd wanted to kiss her so badly, had managed to pull back only because he was afraid she wasn't ready. And above all, Jake didn't want to scare her off.

As the folds became more difficult, Jake didn't have to pretend to be confused. But he followed her directions as best he could, and she continued to direct his hands with her own. Jake wasn't sure how he'd remember to do this in order to teach Callie. Luana's nearness was such a distraction, he couldn't count on remembering any of the instructions. He'd have to stop at a bookstore and hope he could find a book with illustrated directions.

Finally, she folded up the tail, tugged gently at the wings, and showed him the bird she had made. When he did the same steps, producing one of his own, he felt a sense of accomplishment almost equal to his satisfaction over his excellent photos. And Luana's praise was enough to make his heart sing.

"I'll never remember how to do another," he told her. "We'll have to do it again."

"Of course."

Luana's reply added to his happiness. She didn't mean to toss him out of her office after making only one bird. She would let him stay and do another.

"I have diagrams to help you remember, too. I prefer to show you without it at the beginning, though. Once you have the technique down, it will serve as a memory guide."

They spent another hour folding, and had a sizeable stack of birds by the time they were done.

Luana put them all into a box when it was time for him to leave.

"I have the paper in here too, for you to practice with, or for when you have the chance to teach Callie. Will she be coming early for the wedding?"

"I doubt it." No need to explain that both Callie and Tommy would be touring until just before the day of the wedding. "But I'll be going back at some point for a short visit before the wedding. If nothing comes up, I'll just take a few days to go over and show her how to do this. I sent her those brochures you gave me, and she was excited by the idea of having the good-luck cranes and displaying them in picture form. She even decided on the picture," he added. "She wants a golden circle with their initials woven into the center of it."

"That sounds very attractive. I'm sure they'll be able to do it. But you realize they will have to have the cranes at least a week before the wedding. They weren't happy with that small a timeframe, either, but I told them you would pay a premium price to have it done on time."

Luana looked up at him through her lashes. He loved the way she did that.

"That's fine. It's just what I would have done." Callie however, would have had a tantrum or cajoled, depending on the mood she was in on that particular day.

Jake bent as he reached to take the box from her. Their hands brushed, and he remembered how soft and gentle her fingers were, their every move a graceful dance. He recalled the warm tear he'd stopped, so like a diamond sparkling on her cheek.

Jake couldn't believe the flights of fancy his mind took these days. But when Luana was this close, he couldn't think straight and his thoughts flew with these romantic notions. Right now, his head was inches from her cheek. He wanted to lean forward that tiny bit and place a kiss there. And then it would be so simple to nibble a trail to her lips. They were sure to be even softer than her fingers. From their first meeting, he'd been fascinated by her full lower lip, more than anxious to explore it.

Jake wondered if his desire showed in his eyes. Luana suddenly pulled away from him, stepping back so quickly, she almost tripped on her feet. Or the hem of her long dress. Whatever the cause, the mood was broken, even as she thanked him again for his gift of the photographs.

Jake accepted the box and settled for giving her a warm smile.

* * *

"I've got a date," Mele called out, hurrying across the store to Luana's floral corner.

Luana was hunched over her worktable, studying floral designs in one of her binders. She and Jake had decided on the style of bouquets for Callie's wedding, but she had not yet made a final decision on the type of flowers.

She straightened now, watching her friend approach.

"The new owner?"

The seafood restaurant where Mele worked had changed owners yet again in the past month, making it the third time in less than six years. The new owner was in his thirties and from Honolulu and Mele had been pining over him since the first day they met.

"I wish." Mele sighed.

"I'm not sure I've seen him. What does he look like?"

Mele gave her a curious look. "You waved to him when he drove by the other day."

Luana shrugged. "I don't remember." The truth was she waved to almost anyone driving through Malino. In such a small place, she just assumed acquaintance. Their main street wasn't exactly a major thoroughfare.

Mele put her hands on her hips and glared. "Where's your mind at these days? How could you forget seeing a guy who looks like that?" Her eyes became dreamy as she described him. "Thick dark hair, fun-loving eyes. Crooked smile. And he's a sharp dresser too."

Luana's cheeks turned pink. Mele's description of her boss carried too many similarities to Jake—thick hair, fun-loving eyes, crooked smile, sharp dresser.

Mele looked hard at Luana's hot face. "Ah-ha! You're not thinking of Kurt at all, are you? It's that client of yours, isn't it? The one planning the wedding for his relative."

Luana took her time answering.

"I do think of him quite a bit, but that's because he can be difficult to work with. It takes up a lot of my time. Especially now, since I'm trying to be nice while he's here waiting. The resort manager told me to be nice to him," she added.

"Sure."

But it was obvious that Mele didn't believe her.

Why was she so determined to create a relationship between them? Luana wanted to get her off the subject. Why had she come rushing in here? Ah . . .

"So, tell me about this date."

Chapter Nine

Luana smiled at the young couple as they entered her office, moving around her desk to offer her hand in greeting. They introduced themselves as they shook her hand.

"I'm Frank Carmanelli. And this is my fiancée, Alyssa Drago."

Luana proffered her own name as she shook Frank's hand. Like so many men's, his hand was quite warm. It was also large, easily encompassing her own. Yet Luana was interested to note that she felt nothing special for that brief moment of time that he held her hand, even though he met her eyes with his. No heat traveled up her arm, igniting her cheeks and turning them red. Interesting little fingers of motion did not travel up her arm and into her spine. Yet Frank Carmanelli was an extremely handsome man, with eyes as blue as the summer sky.

Luana considered the possibility that there was no reaction because she knew he was taken. He and Alyssa were there looking over the resort; they wanted to be married there next summer.

Luana had a long and pleasant conversation with them, talking about the various possibilities for their wedding. But once they left, Luana returned to that brief moment of physical contact and her reaction to it. Or her non-reaction.

She had been trying to tell herself that the powerful physical reaction she experienced when Jake touched her had to do with his extreme good looks. But if it was just a physical reaction based on his appearance, Frank's firm male grip should have elicited a similar response. His hand felt good. It was quite warm. He took her hand in a firm handshake. He was terribly attractive. He even had beautiful blue eyes. Not as beautiful as Jake's, but close. Jake's were a more crystalline blue, almost like blue topaz.

Yes, odd she hadn't realized it earlier. No wonder she found his eyes so appealing. Blue topaz was her birthstone, and had always been her favorite of the colored gemstones.

With a sigh, Luana reached for the ringing telephone. She was as far as ever from solving the enigma of Jake Lawrence. And she was afraid to pursue the matter too intensely—in case she came to a conclusion she would rather avoid.

Jake's head peeked around the door frame. Luana hadn't realized until she saw his attractive face how much she looked forward to his unexpected visits. He seemed to enjoy surprising her with little treats, or just stopping in to say hello.

"Aloha."

Luana smiled a welcome. "Aloha yourself."

Jake stepped into the room. In his hands was the now-familiar tray with its basket of napkin-wrapped treats, and a pot of Kona coffee.

"You know, if I end up gaining ten pounds this month, it's all going to be your fault."

Jake shrugged. "You have a long ways to go before anyone can call you fat, Luana. Just enjoy." He handed her one of the coffee cups. "I just hope I'm getting you into the habit of eating breakfast. That's very important for your health."

"Yeah, I know. You need fuel for your body to work all day. What, were you born on a farm or something?"

Luana sat back, finding she really enjoyed the Portuguese sweet roll he'd brought. Perhaps he was getting her used to eating breakfast after all.

"Actually, I *was* born on a farm."

Luana was surprised by the personal information Jake suddenly provided. She'd just been making conversation, not actually asking. And here he was, finally telling her something about himself.

"Is that so? But you couldn't wait to get off the farm, huh?" She knew he was a city boy. Man, she corrected, her cheeks flushing pink at the thought. City man. He'd mentioned it once before. He said so little about himself, she remembered every little detail.

Jake sat with his hip on the corner of her desk. He looked quite comfortable there as he sipped his coffee, his eyes sparkling with amusement as he watched her.

"It was Dad who couldn't wait to get off the farm. He was more interested in developing new seed strains than in doing the actual growing."

Luana was almost afraid to comment, wondering if her overt interest would make him clam up. In the time she'd known him, he'd done a skillful job of keeping the conversation off his personal life.

"And is he happily developing seeds these days?"

"Yes, he is." Jake grinned. "Nothing makes him happier than sitting in his lab and tinkering."

"I take it that isn't what interests you, however."

Jake turned his head slightly so that he was looking into her eyes.

"Why do you say that?"

"I don't know. You just don't strike me as the scientific type. I see you in a more people-oriented profession."

Jake watched her, an almost mysterious smile on his lips. His dimples flashed and hid with his changing expression.

"Interesting."

The word was uttered so softly, Luana wasn't even sure he'd said it. But then he gave her a wry grin. Only one dimple showed, on the left.

"I'm a lawyer, you know."

Luana couldn't have been more surprised if he'd said he was an undertaker.

"A lawyer?"

"Would you say that was a people-oriented profession?" His eyes danced with amusement. "We attorneys get a bad rap these days, but we can be very nice guys."

Luana didn't know what to say.

Jake laughed. "That was your cue to agree that I'm a nice guy."

Luana twisted her lips as she considered. "Sounds to me like you're fishing for compliments."

His eyes widened, then pleaded with her. He could look so boyishly handsome, Luana had to concede.

"Well, you do bring me coffee."

"And sweet rolls. Don't forget the sweet rolls."

"True." Luana laughed. "Okay. I guess you're a pretty nice guy. For a lawyer."

To her delight, Jake laughed.

"Finally. You're a tough woman to win over, Luana."

He straightened away from the desk, moving around to sit in one of the chairs positioned before it. "I came in to say good-bye."

Luana glanced up, fleeting alarm quickly replaced by what she hoped was a generic look of interest. The bite of roll she'd just taken into her mouth felt like sawdust, and she swallowed hard trying to persuade it to go down her throat. She treated the coughing that followed with a sip of coffee.

Although Jake jumped up and patted her back, she didn't thank him. She didn't say anything, waiting for him to say more. The tightness across her chest chagrined her more than the fact that he was leaving.

"I have to go back to the mainland for a few days."

He continued to hover beside her chair, as though fearing she might start to choke once more.

"Check in at the office, check in with the bride and groom. . . ."

"Good." Luana was glad to hear her voice come out in a normal tone. She'd never been one to lose her composure, but Jake Lawrence certainly was able to achieve that purpose. With little or no effort.

"I also have to teach Callie to make those cranes."

His voice was soft and low, bringing back intimate memories of their time together, folding the little birds. Luana wished he would come to her office again, asking for help making the origami figures. Sitting together, their heads almost touching, had been a joy.

"I'll be back by the end of the week."

Luana heard a promise in the quiet words. He was still on her side of the desk, leaning against the corner, one long leg crossed over the other in a casual manner. He folded his arms over his chest and peered down at her in a mock-stern manner.

"I hope you remember to have breakfast while I'm gone."

Luana hopped up from her chair. At least standing, she didn't feel so small beside him, so much in need of his comfort and protection. And she could put a little more distance between them. Such basic feelings he aroused! She wouldn't have believed she could be such a ninny. She'd always felt she was a modern, independent woman. How could he come into her life and cause such discombobulation by his mere presence?

"I guess I'll be seeing you soon then. Aloha."

She heard the softening of her voice, the promise. Hoping to temper it somewhat, she held her hand out, ready to shake in a businesslike manner.

To her surprise, he had no intention of saying good-bye in such a conventional fashion. He casually uncrossed his legs, pushing away from the desk. Then he stepped up close, invading her space. She could feel the heat of his body, so much larger than her own. His head drew closer, lower.

He's going to kiss me! Luana didn't know whether to panic, or remain calm. Her heart, however, took the decision from her by increasing its pace tenfold. And her treacherous mind whispered, *Finally!*

Luana stared at Jake as he came ever closer. She couldn't have moved away if she'd wanted to. She was immobile, the way she would be in a dream. That's what this was. A dream. She must still be asleep, thinking of Jake coming into her office the way he often did. He was such a handsome man, who wouldn't dream of a kiss? Especially someone imbued with fairy tales like "Sleeping Beauty" as a child.

Jake's face drew ever closer. Was he moving in slow motion, or did it just seem that way? Another reason to think she was dreaming. No one could move that slowly. Could they? Could he?

Then his breath fanned her cheek. A delicious scent of coffee and—lime? perhaps even mint?—tickled her nose. She could see herself reflected in his eyes, the glorious blue color filling her vision. Her dreams were painted with color, but she didn't ever remember having one with aromatherapy aspects.

Then his lips touched hers. Softly, gently, with a touch so light she might have imagined it, he reverently kissed her lower lip. But that heat. That was real; she was sure of it.

His lips touched hers again. This time the pressure was certain. The initial softness grew harder as the kiss deepened.

Luana sighed with pleasure. What a delicious feeling. He tasted of sweetened coffee, and smelled of the outdoors.

Then his hands brushed her shoulders, slipped down her arms, and he stepped away from her. It was over.

Luana stared at him, still dazed. It was over?

He smiled at her, his clear blue eyes twinkling. He knew what she was thinking!

Luana felt her face turn hot and knew it must be red. She took a step back, bumping into her chair, almost falling into the seat. She looked up at him with what she hoped wasn't a loopy smile.

"Well. I guess I'll, uh, see you again soon."

She ran her tongue nervously over her lower lip. The way his eyes latched onto the small movement made her quickly stop. She reached for a pen and fumbled with it as she tried to position it correctly, as though she planned to make a note.

"I'll, uh, be sure everything is set up—so the wedding will go smoothly."

"You do that."

Jake watched her for a moment, then moved around the desk. His step seemed reluctant as he headed toward the door.

He stopped on the threshold, turning to face her. His voice was a mere breath of sound, but filled with promise. "Aloha."

With that he was gone. Luana watched the doorway for several minutes, rolling the pen between her fingers. Then she let it fall onto her desk and dropped her head into her hands. What on earth was she going to do? She had fallen in love with Jake Lawrence, of the clear blue eyes and the gentle good-bye kiss. Jake Lawrence, a rich lawyer from the mainland, a man who lived in a big mainland city.

Tears gathered in her eyes, but Luana refused to let them fall. She'd have to handle this. She didn't know how, but she would get through it. Two people who enjoyed each other's company, but had none of the big things in common—how could a couple like that expect any happiness?

Luana lifted her head, blinked back any remaining tears, and turned off her computer. It was time to return to Malino. There she could recoup her spirit. There, she could figure out what to do.

Jake flew home, called in at his office, and spent a night in his own bed. He should have slept like a baby, but instead he spent a restless night wondering why he'd never gotten a house. The apartment was one of the best the city had to offer; the location was convenient and his friends always commented on its stylish and tasteful decor.

But at the moment he was seeing it through Luana's eyes. In that context, the apartment seemed cold, the decor stiff and impersonal. Someone like Luana needed a real home, a house, with decorations specially chosen by the owners, and a yard where she could grow flowers. The flowers here would be different from the ones in the Islands. Would she mind?

He didn't know when he'd made the decision, but he knew that he didn't want to continue his lonely days of being a workaholic. He wanted Luana in his life permanently, wanted to enjoy the companionship he'd found with her on a daily basis.

The thought made Jack smile in the deep darkness of his bedroom. He'd ask her to marry him, he decided. As soon as he got back, he'd find some impossibly romantic spot, invite her to view it with him, and pop the question.

That decided, he dropped off the sleep, dreaming gentle dreams of Luana as a bride.

He felt rested the next morning, and wished he could fly right back to Hawaii. But he had another plane to catch, one heading to Denver, and a meeting with Callie.

The short flight was worse than the long night. He was haunted by thoughts of Luana and the good-bye kiss he'd stolen from her. He could still feel her in his arms; she was a tall woman, and filled his embrace in a way none of the lean models he often dated ever had. She'd melted against him, soft and yielding, but only for a moment. Then she'd stiffened and pulled away.

But for that brief moment when their lips touched . . . That had been special. More than special. She smelled like a rare tropical blossom, and she tasted like one too. Her mouth had been sweeter than a mango, lighter than the papaya he'd had with his breakfast. And her touch on his arms, tentative as it was, brought such a surge of desire he tried not to bring it to mind.

"Jake!"

Callie was staring at him, an odd expression on her pretty young face.

As he'd told Luana, Callie was enamored of the idea of the lucky cranes. She'd gathered together her backup singers and anyone else from her entourage who was willing to learn the technique along with her. Stacey, her best friend, choreographer, and maid of honor, had flown in from LA to join them.

"This is such fun," Stacey commented, her fingers fumbling with the gold paper. "Even though I am such a klutz. Maybe I should have let Roy come along."

Callie looked up from the paper she had carefully folded. Unlike Stacey, Callie had taken to the technique, finding the folding easier than some of her friends.

"Did he want to come? None of the guys on the tour wanted to do it. I asked them." Her lips tipped into a dreamy smile. "I'll bet Tommy would have done it, though."

Stacey was still struggling with her paper. "I couldn't believe it. Can you just imagine him doing this? I can't. But he made a big deal out of me leaving without him. You'd think I was going on a two-week vacation and leaving him behind."

"Maybe we'll be having another wedding soon." Callie

winked at her friend. "Sounds like he can't live without you."

Stacey stopped fighting with the gold paper. "Oh, my gosh. Maybe that's it." Her cheeks grew pink as her eyes widened with discovery. In her hands, the gold paper crinkled into a crumbled ball.

The other women gushed over this romantic possibility while Jake thought he finally understood the derivation of the term "hen party." What a noise they made!

He let his mind wander back to Luana, who had taught him how to make the cranes he was now attempting to teach the women to make. He could almost feel the pressure of her smooth brown fingers moving over his as she showed him the proper folds. He recalled the tickle of her hair on his nose, the delicious scent that rose from her warm body.

That was when Callie began calling to him.

"Earth to Jake."

Pulled back to the hotel suite by Callie's insistent voice and the laughter of the others, Jake grinned sheepishly at his sister.

"Sorry. My mind was wandering."

"I guess."

She cast a quizzical look at him. "I'm just wondering who it is that's making it wander. You have that look, Jake."

Her friends all laughed at Jake's reaction, which was to deny everything and direct them all to the next step. He wasn't about to pursue *that* comment. Even if he knew it to be true.

"Now pay attention; this is complicated. You have to open the sides here, to make it into a diamond shape."

As he demonstrated, he kept his eyes on the diagrams

Luana had provided. If he concentrated hard enough, he could probably keep his mind on the origami and off Luana. And keep Callie's speculative looks at bay. He didn't want to share his dreams of the future with anyone until he had a chance to share them with Luana.

"I have to thank you for all you're doing for Tommy and me, Jake." Callie worked carefully to make her crane, but she didn't have to concentrate as hard as some of the others. As she folded the gold paper, she smiled her gratitude over at her half-brother. "I think our wedding is going to be fantastic."

Jake shrugged off her thanks but agreed about the wedding.

"Are you done with that step?"

He looked around, but several of the women were still folding. Or frowning at the paper in their hands in a manner that did not bode well. Stacey had taken another sheet of paper, and one of the other girls was guiding her through the earlier steps. Jake got up, moving about the luxurious room to supervise. When they were all done and working on the next step together, he finally answered Callie.

"It's not me that's making this wedding special, you know. It's Luana Young, the wedding coordinator at the resort. She's doing a great job."

Callie glanced up with interest. "Is that so?" Her look turned speculative. "So what does this Luana Young look like, Jake?"

She watched Jake carefully as he described the tall, graceful wedding coordinator. Jake would have been more careful if he'd noticed; he was so involved in his description of Luana's fine personality that he barely remembered to demonstrate the next origami fold.

When Jake finally left late that afternoon, Callie hugged him tightly.

"Thanks for everything, Jake. And I'm so glad you're actually taking a vacation while you're there. Enjoy yourself." She stepped back and her eyes danced over him. "You look good in a tan, big brother. Real good."

"You've been a real grump lately, Luana."

Luana and Mele sat on the floor in Luana's room, a fan moving the hot air around them. On this languid Sunday afternoon, they could have been teenagers again, playing music and talking about guys. Luana had just scolded Mele for dropping a CD. Mele would have understood if she'd scratched the disk by dropping it on the floor. But it had fallen gently on one of the pillows they were lounging on, nothing that should have aroused Luana's severe reaction.

"Maybe you're not getting enough sleep," Mele continued. "Are you still dating that guy every night?"

Luana frowned heavily. "I have *not* been a grump."

She heard her bad-tempered response and groaned.

"Okay, maybe I have." She rolled from her stomach to a sitting position. "Sorry."

Mele accepted her apology with grace.

Luana admitted to experiencing some insomnia as she pushed the jewel boxes in her hands back into the box on the floor between them. She leaned back against the bed, throwing her head back over the mattress.

"I don't know what's wrong with me lately. I just have the blahs, I guess. I don't mean to take it out on you."

Luana felt guilty that she wasn't admitting the truth to her good friend. She missed Jake, that's what was making her grumpy. But she was reluctant to tell Mele that.

"So . . ." Mele settled herself against the bed as well,

stretching out her legs before her and crossing them at the ankles. "Still going out every night? Missing a lot of sleep?"

Unconsciously, Luana imitated Mele's posture, crossing her ankles.

"I have *not* been going out every night, just having some trouble sleeping."

She decided to ignore Mele's knowing "ah-ha."

"And I'm not dating him, by the way. I told you it was a business thing."

"Sure."

Mele's grin made Luana frown. This was another thing Luana didn't understand. She'd always shared feelings about boyfriends with Mele before. Yet Jake was too special; she wanted to hold her memories of him close to her heart.

"Anyway, he went back to the mainland."

"I thought he was staying until the wedding?"

"I assumed he was." Luana shrugged. "He went to consult with the bride. And teach her how to make origami cranes."

"Ahh." Mele leaned forward, stifling a giggle. She had always found the thought of the virile man Luana described making origami figures funny. "Do you think he'll tell you more about her when he comes back?"

"The bride? I don't know. Probably not."

Luana reached for the portable CD player, removing the disk that had just finished and inserting another. Darlene Ahuna's full voice filled the room as she began "That's the Hawaiian in Me." Both women were silent for a few minutes as they listened.

"That's such an old song," Mele said, reaching for the button that would move to the next track.

But Luana was reluctant, stopping her hand. She wanted to hear the sentimental song, to remind herself of her heritage, of all the reasons why Jake was so wrong for her.

"Sometimes it's good to hear these old songs. This is one of my grandmother's favorites. And swing is back, you know."

Mele's eyes questioned her, but neither of them said a word as the song played out.

As the haunting piano accompaniment of "Ka Pili 'Oe" began, Luana sank down lower against the bed, listening. She was almost flat on the floor now.

Mele frowned at her friend. "I think maybe you're working too hard," she said. "All those weddings and all. It's got to be depressing, doing all that planning and not being able to plan your own."

Luana's eyes widened in surprise. She sat back up.

"You may be right." Her brows drew together as she considered this new idea. "It was such a lot of fun in the beginning, helping couples plan wonderful weddings. The brides get so excited. And then seeing them beforehand, all nervous and happy . . ." She heaved a giant sigh. "I want to have a special wedding myself one day. And who knows *when* that might be."

"Well, if you play your cards right, you might be able to have a double wedding with your mystery bride," Mele suggested with a laugh.

Luana threw a pillow at her, then had to fend off the one Mele launched back at her. Soon they were both laughing, pillows flying between them. Finally, Luana leaned back against the bed, stuffing one of the pillows behind her head.

"I keep telling you, it's not that kind of relationship."

"Okay." Mele nodded but Luana knew she'd go on believing what she wanted.

"He's really good-looking and I like being with him."

Luana stopped Mele before she could pitch in with an "I knew it."

"But there are just too many problems."

Mele didn't want to give in so easily. "Like what?" she asked.

"Just everything," Luana retorted. "He's a tourist, Mele, staying in one of the nicest resorts on the island. For a month! You know how expensive that is?"

Mele nodded. "I wouldn't mind a husband who had money."

"The concept is nice, but think about it. It's not just that he has money. And he does, because this wedding is going to cost a small fortune, and he acts like it's nothing. We're talking a complete difference in lifestyles here. And I'm sure he's a city boy through and through."

"Well, you're no city girl." Mele laughed. "I guess that's another one of your problems."

Luana wasn't laughing. "Definitely. I've been to Honolulu a couple of times, but I'm a small-town country girl. Like you. What would people like us do in a big city, Mele?"

Mele shrugged. Then a smile broke. "Go shopping!"

This time Luana had to laugh too. She was glad she had Mele here to help pull her out of her attack of the doldrums.

"You know, I was watching that entertainment show on TV last night." Mele's voice was thoughtful. "They had some footage from this actor's wedding. Some big action-hero guy. Not my kind of movies." She dismissed the big-budget blockbusters with a wave of her hand. "But, Luana, he flew all his guests to this little island in the Caribbean. They didn't know what they were going there for, just some kind of party. It was to keep the paparazzi away. Does that remind of you anything?"

Luana sighed. Mele was captivated by the mystery surrounding the Smith wedding. She brought it up whenever they were together, eager to learn more about the strange arrangement.

"Honestly, Mele, you need to read some murder mysteries so you can assuage this passion of yours to discover all the answers." Luana shook her head. "I don't think it's the same thing at all."

Was it? Luana did pause, determined to consider it later, at her leisure. Anyway, even if it was similar, she would be honor-bound to keep it to herself. Even from a friend as close as Mele. She'd promised Jake. And the hotel.

"Okay, maybe it's not the same." It was Mele's turn to sigh. "But wouldn't it be exciting if it was?"

They sat for a moment, letting the fan blow over their damp faces, listening to the music. Darlene Ahuna's voice slid effortlessly into the high notes of "Kaua'i Beauty." It was a typical, quiet Malino afternoon.

"You know nothing exciting ever happens around here."

Another sigh from Mele was her friend's only agreement.

Chapter Ten

Jake returned to Kukui Wana'ao with a mound of gold paper cranes and an anticipation so intense it frightened him. First thing in the morning he would drop in on Luana. The thought alone was enough to increase his heart rate. Perhaps he would be able to steal another kiss.

As he set the box of cranes on the desk in his room, he wished it was earlier in the day. But at least he had these to give her tomorrow. He opened the box and stared at its glittering contents. It was nowhere near the one thousand and one needed for the good-luck picture, but still, there were several hundred gold paper cranes to give to the custom designer. Callie would have her special, framed-and-mounted work of art, and be able to say that she and her friends had made many of the cranes.

As Jake returned the lid to the box, he anticipated the smile that would warm Luana's eyes when she saw the cranes. And he would have them in her hands the requisite week before the wedding date.

He thought back to the day he'd taught Callie and her friends to make the cranes. Callie had accused him of being distracted, of having "that look." He'd ignored her at the time, but he knew she thought he was in love.

Jake had never been in love, but he felt sure this was it. He'd never felt quite this way about any other woman. Their time together always flew by, pleasant conversation and mutually enjoyable activities filling the hours until they seemed like merely an instant. Luana filled his mind, his senses. She aroused primitive instincts in him; he wanted to protect her, to make her happy, to hold her close forever. That had to mean love.

For the first time in his life, the thought of being in love didn't scare him. In fact, it made him unbelievably happy.

With a smile, Jake pulled out his swimming clothes. He had plenty of time for a swim before dinner. He was whistling as he headed for the elevator.

Jack awoke early the next morning, anticipating his reunion with Luana. He placed the room service order for breakfast, then took off for an early swim. He'd be back in plenty of time to change and collect their breakfast rolls and coffee.

Jake found himself holding his breath as he approached the door to Luana's office. He'd so looked forward to seeing her again. But what if her welcome was less than he'd hoped?

He needn't have worried. Luana looked up as soon as he stepped into her doorway, as if she sensed his presence. He knew he'd approached silently as the hotel lobby was covered with a thick carpet that absorbed any sound of footsteps. Her face lit up when she saw him, a smile touching not only her lips, but her entire face.

Jake wanted to leap over her desk and pull her into his arms. But he didn't want to scare her, so he knew he'd have to practice restraint. He wondered how long he'd have to coddle her with breakfast treats before he could tell her how he felt.

"Good morning, Luana." He set the tray on her desk, but neither of them even gave it a glance. "I brought some coffee and rolls."

"Aloha, Jake. How thoughtful of you."

The two of them stood, one on either side of the desk, staring into each other's eyes. Luana seemed almost in a trance, and Jake was so thrilled he wanted more desperately than ever to kiss her again.

"I missed you," Jake ventured.

Luana seemed pleased to hear it. A look of pleasant surprise passed over her, then her eyes were drawn down to his mouth. He watched with fascination as the tip of her tongue ventured out, running along the edge of her upper lip.

Jake shifted uncomfortably from one foot to the other, and his movement seemed to break the hypnotic spell. It also pulled a reply from Luana.

"I, uh, missed you too."

Unfortunately, she didn't sound as though she really meant it. Jake wondered if she just didn't want to admit it. Yes, he liked that thought. She was so different from any other woman he'd ever known. His usual date would have purred the line at him, adding a lingering touch to his arm or his face. Just his luck he would fall for such a reticent young woman, too shy to speak out about her feelings.

The initial spell broken, Jake decided it was time for breakfast.

He offered the basket of rolls to Luana and was not surprised when she refused them. He wasn't sure he had any appetite himself after the intensity of seeing her again. He had to get her beyond this embarrassment she felt about expressing her emotions. If he could only gather her up and greet her properly—with hugs and kisses—they would be past all this. It was all so juvenile, yet he knew that Luana was just not ready to acknowledge what they had. He'd have to give her more time.

So he busied himself with pouring the coffee.

"I have a box of gold paper cranes for you. I didn't count them, but there are several hundred. Callie had all her girlfriends over to help, and they made a lot of them. Callie was very good at it too. She made two for each one made by everyone else."

Luana was smiling at him.

"Just you and Callie and all her girlfriends, huh?"

Her teasing tone warmed his heart.

"Hey, I feel lucky to have survived it." His aggrieved tone made Luana laugh.

Then his demeanor turned serious. "I still missed you."

Luana couldn't avoid the intimate tone of his declaration. She'd missed him too, of course, but she wasn't sure she was ready to admit it so freely. The intensity of the emotions she'd felt when she spotted him in her door were too raw, too scary. What they had between them was no summer fling. That would have been easy to disdain. But she didn't know if she was brave enough to accept what he seemed to be hinting at. The gulf between them was still huge. He still hadn't told her about himself, or his family.

Luana set down her coffee cup.

"So, where are the cranes? I'll have to get them over to the design company right away."

Jake nodded. "I couldn't manage both the box and the tray, and my stomach won."

Luana watched him grin. The left side of his mouth quirked up a little higher than the other. His eyes danced with mischief and laughter. And those impish dimples gave him a boyish look, even though he was all man.

Luana swallowed. How could she ever have thought him shallow? He was kind and sensitive, polite and understanding, playful and insightful. And he had depths she had still to explore.

"I'll bring them down as soon as we finish." He offered the basket once again. "Are you sure you don't want something to eat?"

Luana shook her head. How could she eat when her stomach was tight as a knot? She wanted to know him better, wanted it with a fierceness that defied logic and residency issues. How long would it be before she no longer cared that he lived in a city three thousand miles away?

Jake brought her out of her introspective mood by asking about the wedding. She was able to offer a true smile then. It was definitely easier to work with him when things were on a business relationship.

"So is everything all set?" he asked. "It's just a week away now."

"Yes." Luana shuffled a few papers and pulled one to the top. "I was speaking to the chef just before you came in. We have the menu all worked out. I think everyone will be pleased. Do you have the final guest figures for us?"

Jake nodded. "One hundred and fifty-five."

"Wonderful." Luana jotted the figure on the menu sheet.

"And we do allow for some dinners over that figure, in case of last-minute arrivals."

Jake didn't mention the impossibility of that in this particular case. It was possible Callie would allow a few more on the chartered plane, but no one was going to crash this party. He'd see to that.

"I've made all the arrangements for the plants and flowers. The room where the ceremony will be held will have what looks like a garden at one end. And the trellis will be covered with passion flower vines and blossoms."

Jake nodded his approval. "Callie will be thrilled."

Luana was glad to hear it. She'd loved the idea, but she still felt the constraints of never having spoken to the bride.

"Can you think of anything else that you want to check on?"

Jake just grinned. "I'd love to drive you and the cranes over to the design studio. Then we can go to the beach afterward."

Luana wasn't sure how he seduced her into agreeing. But within the hour, they were driving down to Kona in his convertible, the wind blowing through their hair, their laughter mixing with the strains of Hawaiian guitars from the radio.

Luana sat on a towel, on the white sands of Hapuna Beach, watching Jake swim. She'd been in the water earlier, but couldn't last as long as he did. She liked swimming alongside him, with his strong strokes breaking the water. She knew he had slowed his normal pace for her, and she was grateful. There was no way she would ever win a race against him, even though she was an excellent swimmer.

She watched him now as he walked from the waves, water streaming off his body. He shook his head as he gained the sandy beach, and she laughed out loud to see him. For not fifty feet down the beach, a golden retriever was doing basically the same thing.

She saw Jake's head come up as he heard her laughter, and he jogged over to her, throwing himself down on her towel.

"Hey!" She was still laughing, but she brushed moisture from her cheek. "You're getting me all wet. That's your towel over there." She pointed to the towel laid out beside hers.

"I like this one."

Jake flashed a grin at her that had her heart beating at twice its usual rate. Flirty, mischievous, boyish—the man could say a thousand things with just one grin.

"Well, then, I'll move."

With graceful movements, she rose to her feet and stepped over his long, damp legs. But before she could put her foot down on the towel, she found herself flat on her back in the sand.

"What . . . ?"

Jake's face loomed above her, still grinning.

"How'd you do that?" She glared at him, but it seemed to have no effect at all.

"Now, this is nice."

He was so close, Luana could barely focus on him. His head rested on his hand, propped up by his elbow, as he lay stretched out beside her. *His* body, she noticed, was still on the towel, while she could feel the gritty sand seeping beneath her suit and prickling her scalp. Well, two could play at that game.

She dug her hands into the sand, holding two fistfuls ready.

"What's nice about it?"

"Well." He glanced leisurely over her face. "It's a beautiful, sunny day. There's a nice breeze, so it's not too hot. And I'm lying on the beach beside the prettiest girl on the island."

"Who's lying in the sand!"

She spoke the first words in a low, sultry voice, but shouted the word "sand" as she raised both hands and emptied them over him. Then she leaped up and raced for the water.

He caught her in the foamy surf, and they both went down in the water. An incoming wave covered them, and they came up laughing and sputtering, coughing up salt water.

"You play dirty," Jake accused her, wiping water from his eyes.

"And you don't?"

He had to concede her point, graciously helping her push her wet and tangled hair back from her face. His hands were so gentle, Luana could almost forgive him for his earlier shenanigans.

They remained in the water for a while, just floating and watching the waves come in. When they headed back to their towels, Jake declared it mealtime, and reached into a cooler he'd brought for cold drinks, sandwiches, and fruit.

"Where did you get all this?" Luana asked, grateful but amazed. There hadn't been that much time between his asking to take her to Kona and their leaving. And they had been together since they left the resort.

Jake almost smirked. "A man has to have some secrets."

Luana raised her brows. "Isn't that supposed to be *my* line?"

His voice gentled to that seductive tone he had that made her heart turn over.

"I just want to take care of you. I've been feeling so good since I started this vacation, I wanted to help you relax too."

Luana had bristled at his words, but felt her reaction soften as he finished. She could see the difference in him since their first meeting. It was more than the physical changes, too, the golden tan he'd acquired, or the way his hair had grown out and achieved more natural streaks. He did seem more relaxed.

"You work too hard, Luana. You need more fun afternoons like this one."

Luana finished her sandwich and crumpled the wrappings into a ball. She hated being told what to do. And it really was none of his concern.

On the other side of the towel, Jake could see Luana closing up on him. Darn, but he thought this casual time together had helped his cause. He was almost ready to tell her how he felt. And now she'd distanced herself from him. Again.

Jake finished his own food slowly, sipping a cola while he watched Luana. He should have known better than to attack her workaholic lifestyle. Hadn't Callie told him he'd been the same way?

Stifling a word or two he didn't want to say in front of Luana, Jake threw his trash into the now empty cooler. He almost groaned as he watched Luana bite into a large peach, then reach up to wipe the juice from her chin. Fantasies of licking away the juice, of kissing her juice-sweetened lips, were almost his undoing.

With a swift movement, Jake stood.

"I think I'll have one more quick dip, then we can go."

He saw Luana's surprise, but he didn't give her time to reply, just headed back into the water. He needed some time alone while she finished that darn peach. Otherwise, he couldn't be held accountable for his actions.

Jake swam through the cool water of a mountain pool. Shaded by the deep green of lush tropical growth, the pool featured a small waterfall and an intimate privacy.

Through the clear water he could see Luana swimming toward him. Her golden-brown skin glistened in the slick dampness, her long dark hair floated around her head like a sailor's dream of a mermaid. As she drifted past him, long strands of her hair trailed over his shoulder. The silken touch wrapped around him, warming him in the cool water.

A bee buzzed at his ear and he flung his head to send it away. Water droplets scattered across the surface of the water, but the sound of the bee only intensified. As the buzzing grew louder, he lost sight of Luana. Then the tropical rain forest and the pool itself dissolved into gray mist and only darkness remained.

Jake pushed himself up, disoriented. He wasn't swimming with Luana in some hidden paradise, just asleep in his bed at the resort. The room was dark, but he could make out the furnishings. He'd taken to sleeping with the drapes open, the sliding glass doors wide; the screen door provided whatever security was necessary on the eighth floor of a luxury resort. The quarter moon had provided a silvery glow to the whole when he'd dropped off to sleep, looking forward happily to the morning and his reunion with Luana. But now the moon was gone, the sky dark, even the stars invisible. Only the sound of the ocean remained the same, the soothing susurration a pleasant counterpoint to his sudden awakening.

He blinked again, but the room remained steeped in dark gray shadows. The pesky bee of his dream still buzzed—

his cell phone, ringing insistently from its place on the small table beside the bed.

Jake grabbed it, punching at the correct button.

"What?" He shouted the word rudely into the phone, but he wasn't feeling especially charitable at the moment.

His caller shouted back.

"Jake! Have you seen the *Starcatcher?*"

"Callie?" Now that he'd identified the caller, he lowered his voice to a conversational level. Darn, but she'd done it again. And this time the brush of dawn hadn't even begun to paint the room.

"Well, have you?"

Jake pushed the bed pillows into a pile under his head. He closed his eyes as he answered.

"Callie, it's the middle of the night here. How could I have seen it? I doubt if any supermarkets are even open yet."

Jake sighed. He didn't know what she was so upset about, but he'd probably have to go out as soon as the stores opened looking for a copy of the tabloid.

"They know about the wedding, Jake."

Jake sat up, wide awake now. "What do you mean they know? How did they find out?"

"That's what I want to know. Those people at the hotel must have told them. That wedding coordinator."

Her voice was indignant. Accusing. Jake pictured the lovely Luana, with her honest, open face. Unfortunately, he could also see Callie, her pretty features clouded by hurt.

"I don't think so." His voice was firm.

"It's got to be them." Her young voice was filled with conviction. "They know what we're wearing, and they know about Reverend Johnston. I want you to sue them,

Jake. You told them before we even started what was required. We can sue."

"I'm not that kind of lawyer." Jake's voice was tired, and not just from lack of sleep.

"Well, you should be. They make lots of money. You must know someone. Lawyers always stick together."

Jake could see Callie, even though she was thousands of miles away. She would be stalking whatever open floor area was offered in tonight's hotel suite—in Phoenix, he thought—like a tiger in a cage. But he came to attention at her next words.

"I want that woman fired. She must have sold the information about the wedding. We should make her give all the money to charity, too."

Her voice broke on what sounded suspiciously like a sob.

"Why does this always happen to me, Jake? Why do people always turn on me?"

Jake felt a pressure in his chest—his heart constricting in sympathy. Poor Callie. Like so many celebrities, she had been burned more than once by those who wanted to be her friend for their own profit.

His voice softened with love for this young girl who had had to grow up at a very young age. "It doesn't *always* happen, Callie. Plenty of people like you for yourself."

He gave her a moment to gather herself before rising to Luana's defense.

"It wasn't her, Callie." Jake's voice was firm. "The hotel has been very discreet. Besides, I didn't tell her who you are. I never gave her your full name—just said the couple would be Mr. and Mrs. Smith. I hated doing it, too, because I like her and she's a trustworthy person. I'm sure of it. But I'd promised you."

But Callie was too upset to listen.

"She could have found out. You said I was your sister, didn't you? How hard could it be to find out Jake Lawrence has a half-sister who's a celebrity?"

The odd thing about Callie was that in her mouth a sentence like that could come out without sounding the least bit pretentious.

Jake combed his fingers through his hair. "I did not tell her you were my sister."

"She could figure that out."

Jake knew he would never convince her in her present mood. Besides, she was probably right. But he knew Luana would not have even tried.

Better to humor Callie and just try to soothe her.

"Did they say where it would be?"

"No."

That should have made her feel better, but her voice was still full of anger. She would not be easy to calm.

"Then it'll still work out okay. You'll have your beautiful wedding here next week. If someone from the hotel had leaked out the information, they would have said where it would be—they'd want the publicity for the hotel."

"Oh, Jake! They aren't going to print that information now." Her voice was filled with exasperation. It was as though suddenly he was the teenager and she the adult. "It would let all the other tabloids know where the wedding is. They want to keep it to themselves. So they can sneak in and get an exclusive."

Jake had to give her credit for creative thinking. Still, it was just the kind of thing those sneaky papers would do. "Maybe."

"No maybe," she retorted. "I'm right."

Jake closed his eyes, trying to get his brain operating. He massaged his neck with his free hand, hoping to get the blood circulating and the little gray cells stimulated. There must be some way to exonerate Luana.

"Who exactly knows about the wedding? And I mean *everyone* you've told. You and Tommy both."

A sudden thought almost made him shout into the phone. "You didn't tell your mother, did you?"

Callie's reply was indignant. "Of course not. I know she'd tell in a heartbeat. I'm not that dumb."

Jake thought it sad, because it was true. Liz was mentally ill, her insane jealousy of her only child's success unnatural.

"Besides, she's in that sanitarium in Connecticut. Dad says she's medicated and doing well. She sings for the other patients. But she couldn't cause this kind of trouble from there anyway. She wouldn't have unsupervised access to a phone."

"So who have you told? Everyone, remember."

She loosed a dramatic sigh.

"The people in the two bands. Tommy's parents. You and Dad. Stacey. Monroe's dad. That's it, honest."

"What about the person who did the gown?"

"No. I told her as little as possible. An approximate date, that's all."

"Could someone in a minor position on one of the tours have found out?"

"No!" Callie was practically shouting now. "I told you, we've been real careful. Even the people who know, don't know where it's going to be or the exact date. We're not going to tell them until they get on the plane. They just know that they have to keep September nineteenth through the twenty-first open."

Jake sighed heavily into the phone.

"Okay. I'll check into it from here. You and Tommy see

if you can learn anything at your ends. Maybe one of the guys told a girlfriend." It was a sudden thought, but sounded better than Callie's idea about Luana being the source of the leak.

Callie made a noncommittal noise at her end.

"It's too late to change it, you know. We'll just have to hire extra security."

"I know. Thanks, Jake."

Jake disconnected, but stayed where he was, propped up in bed, the back of his head flat against the wall. He hated to hear Callie so dejected when this should be a happy time of anticipation. But it couldn't have been Luana. He'd bet his life on it. She wasn't that kind of person. She would never sell out one of her brides for her own self-gain.

And besides . . . she didn't know enough to have told.

Chapter Eleven

Before Luana even reached her office that morning, she received an urgent message requesting her presence in the general manager's office. Luana's stomach immediately filled with butterflies. This was the equivalent of a childhood summons to the principal's office. What could she have done?

Then she scolded herself. Why did she assume it was something bad? Perhaps he wanted to congratulate her for a job well done. Or ask her to take particular care of another client. Comforted by this thought, Luana entered the elevator.

Any soothing feelings engendered by her pep talk soared from the large windows opposite when she was shown into Mr. Grantham's office. Jake was there too, and both men wore serious expressions. This would not be a good news session.

"Luana." Mr. Grantham nodded a greeting. "You know Mr. Lawrence. Have a seat, please."

Mr. Grantham gestured toward a chair before his desk. The smile she'd summoned for her entrance disappeared as she looked from Mr. Grantham to Jake. Jake smiled, but it was not the warm welcome she expected. His lips curved upward, and his eyes seemed to be offering her support. But his overall demeanor remained grave.

"Luana," Mr. Grantham began, and she swung her gaze back to him. "When you accepted this job I emphasized the fact that all information you received about hotel guests was confidential. We pride ourselves on protecting the privacy of our guests."

Luana nodded, not yet sure of where this was going. "Yes, sir. And I've been very careful to keep all information I receive private."

"Mr. Lawrence has been working with you on a wedding that demands a higher degree of privacy than most."

Luana glanced at Jake. She could see that he was tense, his lips tight. He was obviously unhappy about something.

"Have you spoken to anyone about the wedding you're planning for Mr. Lawrence?"

Luana began to shake her head before he'd even finished speaking. "I would never do that."

"You didn't tell anyone? Not your parents, your brother, your best girlfriend?"

Jake's voice was more intense than she'd ever heard it.

She shook her head again. "If I speak about my work here, I do so in very general terms. I might tell someone that I'm planning a sunset wedding on a cliff overlooking the beach. I couldn't say much of anything about Ja—, ah, Mr. Lawrence's wedding, because I don't know anything personal about the couple." She paused. "I think that's what

I told my girlfriend, actually." Her eyes met Jake's. She wouldn't plead with him if there was some problem. He'd have to believe her. She set her chin at a challenging angle. "Right after your first visit I told her a crazy man wanted me to plan a wedding and wouldn't tell me anything about the couple."

Jake frowned. He'd noted the set of her chin before she called him crazy. His lips quivered, anxious to smile. Until he processed what she'd said.

"Did you tell her anything more than that?"

"I don't *know* anything more than that."

Jake could see a stubbornness arise as she continued to stare at him.

"Did you mention my name?"

As Callie had pointed out, anyone with curiosity and a little time for research could discover that entertainment attorney Jake Lawrence was the half-brother of Callie Law.

The question seemed to surprise Luana, who took a moment to think.

"I don't think so. I told her about taking you to some Aloha Festival events, but if I mentioned you by name, I would have just called you Jake."

He saw her eyes slide toward the general manager as she spoke of taking him out, and wondered if there was a no-dating-the-guests policy. He smiled at Mr. Grantham.

"Luana was gracious enough to give up some of her time when I expressed an interest in Hawaiian music. She took me to some extraordinary performances I may not have found on my own. Your personnel here are exceptional in catering to the whims of the guests."

Mr. Grantham returned Jake's smile, expressing his delight in Luana's excellent service and in Mr. Lawrence's satisfaction with the resort. They shook hands all around and Luana left. Jake wanted to follow immediately, but he still had things to settle with Grantham.

Therefore, it was a half hour later when he arrived at Luana's office. She sat stiffly behind her desk, greeting him with tight lips and glaring eyes. She felt she'd been accused of something, without quite knowing what.

"What was that all about?"

Jake seated himself in his usual chair, and wished he'd had time to get some rolls and coffee. It might not have softened up Luana's attitude, but he could have used the caffeine.

"Word has leaked out about the wedding."

Luana's eyebrows rose. "And this has what to do with me?"

He winced at the acid in her voice. "Nothing, Luana. I know it wasn't you. But I had to cover all possibilities, and you are one of them." He ran his fingers through his hair. "Callie called before sunrise, practically crying because word has gotten out. She wants to sue the hotel—probably because she just wants to do *something*. She's positive no one at her end could have done it."

His gaze jumped from her frozen face to her fidgeting fingers. Perhaps she wasn't as cool as she was trying to appear. He tried again.

"Luana, I know you didn't do it."

"You're darn right. You should have trusted that I wouldn't have, even if I did have any information about your precious wedding. I deserved better than a confrontation in my boss's office, Jake."

Jake shifted his eyes away from her. She was right. He should have talked to her first. Alone. But that would have meant waiting to speak to Grantham, and it was essential to get to him as early as possible. That played up the urgency of his case, and would be important if a lawsuit ever did come into play.

Jake sighed. "I did what I could. I told him how great you've been."

"You did." She bowed her head slightly to affirm his glowing report. "But you also interrogated me about my family and friends."

Jake ran his fingers through his hair, wishing again for a cup of coffee. "I have to cover every possibility. Callie wants to sue the resort. She wanted you fired. She was upset, and rightly so, but I told her I had every faith in you."

Jake looked again at the woman he loved. He hoped she could see the pleading in his eyes. "I never believed you were involved, Luana. You have to believe me."

Luana continued to stare at some papers on her desk. He knew she wasn't reading them. He doubted she even saw them. She just didn't want to look at him.

"I had to 'interrogate' you, as you call it, to be sure someone else didn't have enough information to discover the truth of this wedding."

Her head shot back up, and she glared at him.

"You asked if I'd told my family and friends about this wedding, Jake, then asked if I'd given anyone your name." She was angry and not trying to hide it. "For goodness sake, Jake, we've been all over the island, introducing you to people. I never told my best friend your name, but *you've* given it to anyone and everyone."

It was Jake's turn to freeze. He'd never given that a moment's consideration. It meant that anyone at all, if they wanted to learn more about him, could have the information that was leaked out.

But no.

"Callie said they didn't say where the wedding would be held, but that they had inside information about the gowns and the minister. Someone I met at a concert wouldn't know those things."

The words "but you do" hung in the air, unspoken but almost tangible.

Jake ran his fingers through his hair. Again. It was a good thing the new hairstyles embodied the unkept look. He needed to move his hands, and his head was the only thing he trusted himself to handle at the moment. Otherwise, he was likely to throw the small vase that decorated Luana's desk, or fling all her papers to the floor.

He sighed.

"It's important for the couple to have their wedding be private, and for that to happen extraordinary measures have to be taken. Now that word is out about the wedding, everything will be that much more difficult."

Luana's eyes sparked with anger. "You don't trust me, Jake. I didn't question you about the identity of Callie, or of Mr. Smith. I still don't know who they are. And I didn't say anything even though you never mentioned your family, or where you live. It bothered me not to know those things about you, but I didn't ask because it seemed important to you that all this remain secretive. I don't really understand, but that's all right. Because I trusted you."

Her voice broke, but she controlled it, along with any tears that might have threatened. Jake almost wished she would storm and rage, cry, throw things. He could handle that. He handled Callie all the time, and she could have tantrums with the best of them.

But Luana retained her control. She'd even lost the anger that had instigated that last outburst. Now she just looked at him with those large beautiful eyes. That look told him he had betrayed her. That she was disappointed in him.

Jake's hand raked through his hair, and he shifted in the chair. He was restless and uncomfortable. He felt guilty, darn it. He shouldn't have to feel guilty. It wasn't his fault.

He tried again to explain.

"Luana, I'm sorry about all this. But I had to get to Grantham as soon as possible. I couldn't wait to speak to you first. I actually got in touch with him as soon as I finished with Callie. He was still asleep."

He couldn't remain seated for another minute. Rising from the chair, he began to pace the small area before her desk.

"If this wedding turns into a circus, there may be a lawsuit involved. And in that case, it's important that I contacted the hotel the moment I discovered the problem. It's just unfortunate that it put you in an awkward position."

Luana wanted to scream, but she took a deep breath and kept her voice at a reasonable level.

"Unfortunate. Awkward."

Luana rose, feeling at a disadvantage being seated while Jake stood before her. She found that concentrating on taking even breaths helped keep her heart from breaking.

"Oh, Jake. If you think that's all it is, then I guess our relationship wasn't what I thought."

She sank back into her chair and pulled some papers forward.

"I think you'd better go."

Jake sighed. He'd explained, he'd pleaded. There was nothing else he could do. Perhaps if he left, it would give her some time to consider his explanations. He'd give her an hour or two.

She kept her head steadfastly down. Even when he

stopped in the doorway, she didn't look up. Sadly, he walked away. He couldn't know that once he was gone, she fled to the ladies' room. She wouldn't allow the tears to fall until she'd closed herself into one of the stalls.

It was too hard to work. Thankfully, because of the part-time status of her job, Luana didn't have to stay at the resort. She just signed herself out, and returned to Malino for the remainder of the morning. She arrived just at the time she knew Mele would be setting up for lunch.

"So you had a fight with your mysterious *haole?*" All the tables were set, and Mele sat at a table at the back of the restaurant, wrapping flatware into napkins to make later setups easier. Luana helped.

"He's not my *haole.*" Luana's eyes were sad. But mostly she was angry. Angry with Jake for not having faith in her integrity, mad at herself for falling in love with him. "And I always knew he was trouble."

Mele took the fork, knife, and spoon Luana held out and rolled them into a napkin. "So what did you fight about?"

Luana heaved a huge sigh. "He thinks I let word leak out about this wedding. Which is ridiculous of course. I don't know anything about it. I mean, I do know all about it. I've set everything up myself. But I don't know the bride or the groom, so I don't know what exactly it is that I'm supposed to have done."

Mele looked thoughtful. "I always said it must be a celebrity thing, what with all the secrecy and all. So who is it?"

Luana shot her a look that had Mele apologizing.

"Sorry."

"Even if I knew I couldn't tell you."

Mele's hands stilled momentarily as she raised incredulous eyes to Luana. "You mean you *still* don't know who the bride and groom are?"

Luana nodded. "I have no idea. He's never said. After our first meetings, I stopped asking. The manager told me he was an important client and I should give him the best service. So I did."

"And you fell for him, too, didn't you?"

Luana refused to admit it. "Of course not. He was just an important client. So I took an interest in showing him around. He was interested in local music, so we went to see some shows. That's all."

Mele stared at her with raised brows, but Luana refused to back down. She held out the next set of flatware until Mele took it from her, then reached for more. Fork, knife, spoon.

"That's all," she insisted. "He was just a client."

She handed another set to Mele, glad of the repetitious nature of the work.

"And now it looks like it might cost me my new job too."

Luana could feel tears anxious to appear, and she blinked them back with fierce determination. She'd cried once already, and that was more than enough. She refused to let Jake Lawrence turn her into a whimpering female.

"You say he blamed you for letting out information about this secret wedding?"

Luana nodded. "And the resort won't want to keep me if they think I'm letting out private information about clients. They made a big deal about that before I started. The guests' privacy is a big issue with them."

"And you didn't say anything about the wedding to anyone, did you?"

"Of course not!"

Luana's voice was so sharp, Mele apologized quickly.

"I know you didn't, I was just making sure. After all, you didn't spill a word to *me*."

Luana knew her friend was trying to coax her into a smile. But she wasn't in the mood.

"You follow these things. Is there a celebrity you've just heard is getting married? In Hawaii?"

Mele pursed her lips as she thought, napkins and flatware temporarily forgotten. "Hmm. Nope. Not that I recall. And I'd remember if they mentioned Hawaii, especially the Big Island."

She resumed her work, taking the utensils that Luana held ready. "That sexy little pop singer Callie Law is supposed to be getting married, but they didn't say where. I just saw it at the supermarket this morning, in one of the tabloids. She's marrying one of the guys from Four-by-Six. Tommy Teague. He is so cute! But that's the only recent wedding announcement I've seen."

Luana went still. She had to make an effort to continue her work, to be casual. Jake might have indirectly accused her of spilling information, but she had not. And she would not do it inadvertently now either.

"Callie Law? Who is she? I've heard of Four-by-Six."

Mele rolled her eyes. "You must be living in a vacuum if you haven't heard of Callie Law. She's the hottest thing since Britney Spears. Young and cute and sexy as all get-out. And she has a great voice too. She started out in country, singing with her mother. I guess her mother's career didn't really go anywhere, but Callie's sure has since she went solo."

Luana made an effort to shrug casually. "Great voice,

huh? I'll have to listen to the radio, see if I can catch one of her songs."

"I'm surprised you know of Four-by-Six when you haven't heard of Callie Law."

Luana was finally able to laugh. "I know all the boy bands. It's my niece. She loves them all—has their pictures taped up all over the walls of her room. She's probably even shown me pictures of Tommy Teague himself."

Mele sighed. "He is definitely the cutest guy in Four-by-Six, so I wouldn't be surprised. I could go for him myself, though he's a little young." Mele rolled another napkin. "It's sad when the rock stars are too young for you."

"They're getting younger all the time," Luana agreed. "How old is Callie Law?"

Mele shrugged. "Eighteen or nineteen. She's young to be getting married. It's probably just one of those show business rumors. Helps her sell tickets, I suppose. Both Callie and Four-by-Six are touring right now."

"What a way to make a living!"

Mele laughed. "I'd love it!"

She rolled another napkin and added it to the pile. "Too bad about the guy, though. I really thought you liked him."

"I do like him. But that's not the same as being in love, Mele." Maybe if she said it often enough, it would prove to be true.

"I guess."

A customer walked in, and Mele got up. "I've got to get to work." She grasped Luana's hand, giving it a squeeze. "You take care now."

Luana returned the squeeze, then rose and left the restaurant through the back door. She walked home slowly, thoughtfully.

Callie Law. A big-time pop star. It had to be Jake's sister. He had used the name Callie for the bride, and she could easily have shortened her name to "Law." Callie Law had a rhythm to it that was missing from Callie Lawrence.

So a tabloid had announced a wedding eminent for Callie Law and Tommy Teague of Four-by-Six. All the other entertainment media would grab onto the announcement and go with it too.

Luana frowned. Jake had sworn more than once that the groom's last name was really Smith. Probably another case of stage names.

Callie Law and Tommy Teague. It would explain a lot. The instant dismissal of a ceremony on the golf course or on the beach. The reason the couple could not make their own arrangements. The insistence on complete privacy, and the use of what she had suspected were false names. The switching of the two names on the hotel bookings. That must have been to frustrate anyone who might suspect.

A small smile played at the corners of Luana's mouth. She might still be mad at Jake. But at least now she understood a lot of what had happened. It was just too bad their relationship could not be salvaged. She enjoyed his company, had loved introducing him to Hawaiian music, hearing his opinions on the various artists. And the physical chemistry—well, there might not be another man on earth who could affect her that way! But, how could he have implied that she might be responsible for leaking information! He should have trusted her.

Luana sighed. Somehow, she would go on.

Her days as a wedding coordinator might be over though, if word got out that she could have leaked information about a celebrity wedding. Even though she hadn't. There wasn't much she could do to counter the claim. All she could do was provide Callie and Tommy with the best wedding in the world.

Luana firmed her lips and set her chin. And she would.

"Luana!"

Luana spent the afternoon working on flower arrangements at her worktable in the rear of the Young's General Store. She had just started cleaning up when she heard the familiar voice call her name. Emma Correa was walking toward her, her face wreathed in a brilliant smile.

"Luana, I need a special flower arrangement. Right away, if possible."

Emma's smile held throughout her request, causing Luana to smile as well. The blissful face of an old friend like Emma was just what she needed to pull her from drab thoughts of Jake and his betrayal.

"You sure are happy today."

"I am. I'm real happy." Emma beamed.

"So what kind of flowers do you want? I have quite a variety in stock right now. Is it for your mother? I heard she's having an exhibit of her paintings at the library in Kohala."

"She is. And that's a good idea; I'll have to remember to send her something. But not today." Emma walked around the table so that she stood beside Luana, leaning in close and lowering her voice. "This is for Matt. And I want it in one of those little bootie vases you have."

Luana almost shouted, catching herself just in time by clamping her hand over her mouth. She lowered her voice to an excited whisper.

"Emma! You're pregnant?"

"Shh. Yes. I just came from the doctor. I want to tell Matt when I get home, and I thought a special bouquet would be nice."

Luana grinned. "I can't disagree with you there. You know that expression we florists have: Say it with flowers."

She hugged her friend before stepping toward the large refrigerator and peering through the glass doors.

"How about some small mums? I have both white and blue, and I could mix in some pink baby carnations."

"That sounds perfect." Emma cast her a hopeful look. "Can you make it up while I wait?"

"Sure." Luana immediately began to gather up the necessary supplies. This good news was just what she needed to get her out of the blahs that had afflicted her recently.

Emma pulled up the stool that Luana kept near her table but rarely used. She settled herself to watch.

"So, what's happening with you and your handsome *haole?*"

Luana was so surprised, she almost dropped the vase.

"What handsome *haole?*"

"Oh, come on now. You know you can't keep secrets in Malino. I heard you were pretty interested in a cute guy who was arranging a wedding for a relative. Sounds kind of strange to me."

Luana sighed. She fitted the oasis to the small bootie-shaped vase and secured it with a narrow piece of florist's tape.

"The whole thing is more than strange. But it's just a business thing."

Emma looked skeptical but just shrugged. "Too bad. Mele seemed to think you were real interested."

"Darn it, I told her there was nothing there."

"Ah, ha. That's it then. You know what Shakespeare said: the lady doth protest too much."

Luana was choosing flowers, cutting stems, and putting them into the vase. Her hands worked quickly, an attractive arrangement forming beneath her talented fingers.

"That looks so nice, Luana. Great idea using pink and blue flowers."

Emma shifted on the wooden stool. "So you don't think he's the one, huh?"

Luana shrugged. "Okay. I'll admit I was interested. He's real good-looking, real polite. Old-fashioned manners." She sighed. "Lots of charm. But I knew right at the beginning that there couldn't be anything between us. He's just at the resort until this wedding—four weeks from the day we met. There wasn't time. And he'll be going back to the mainland." She sighed. "Next week."

Emma's voice was thoughtful. "Matt and I knew each other forever, of course. But that doesn't mean I don't believe in love at first sight. I kept looking for that, actually, and almost missed what was right there in front of me."

"It's just a business relationship, Emma."

Luana took a white bow from a drawer in the table, attached it to a small stick, and stuck it into the arrangement.

"Voila!"

She turned the vase toward Emma.

"It's perfect!" Emma hopped off the stool and gave Luana a hug. She lowered her voice, leaning in close once more. "And don't tell anybody. I'm telling Matt tonight, then we'll tell my mom. By tomorrow, I guess everyone in town will know."

She and Luana both laughed.

"But seriously, Luana . . . Don't let some disagreement get in the way of your happiness if you really like him. I almost lost Matt because I was too blind to see what I had. I was looking for stars and fireworks, and you know, that's just not always it. Sometimes love is gentler, but it's always the most important thing of all."

"Oh, Jake can provide plenty of fireworks," Luana told

her. She couldn't help but recall the way she felt whenever he touched her. And his kiss . . . She didn't remember any stars or fireworks, but darn, that kiss had been special.

Emma grinned. "Don't worry about him leaving. If it's right for you, he'll be back."

"I don't know, Emma. It's a trust thing. He thinks I might be responsible for releasing some confidential information. I couldn't believe he would even consider it."

"I'm sorry." She gave Luana another hug before picking up her vase. "I've got to go. I'll think about you. Keep in touch."

Luana watched her go, considering her words. She didn't know how much of what Emma said might be true, but she certainly appreciated her trust. In the gossipy, small-town world of Malino, Emma never doubted that Luana would keep word of the new baby to herself.

Chapter Twelve

"A rental car, Jake? How cute."

Jake met Callie, Tommy, and their guests at the Keahole Airport in Kona. Tour buses had been hired to transport the guests from the chartered plane to the resort, but Callie and Tommy were riding with Jake in his convertible. The elder Mr. Lawrence had decided to take the bus, as the family representative.

Callie threw herself into the backseat, pulling Tommy in after her. "Don't they have limos in this place?"

"Sure they do. But you're trying to travel incognito, remember? That's why I have the top up. You wouldn't want some teenage girl to see the two of you and start a riot, would you?"

Tommy laughed. "Just enjoy it, Callie. We'll live like ordinary people for a few days."

Jake laughed too. "Maybe for a day and a half. Tomorrow morning you have to go get the license, and I don't know if we'll be able to keep it a secret after that. Though you'll be using Calista Lawrence and Thomas T. Smith for the license, so that might help. But I still want you to wait until the last moment to get it."

Jake frowned in concern. "I hired more security people, so I hope things will go well. The resort promised to co-operate, and to put on extra security staff as well. They'll be very helpful, hoping to prove that they weren't involved in the leak."

"That's great," Callie said. "But I forgot to tell you. We found the leak. It was Stacey's sleazy boyfriend, can you imagine? She had told him a little and he figured out more by eavesdropping on our phone calls. Then he was stupid enough to buy an expensive new truck last week. That's how she figured it out. Of course, they're through."

Jake felt a tightening around his heart. All the trouble he'd gone through with the resort and the extra arrangements, formulating plans in case they were inundated with reporters and paparazzi. All the cold looks and stiff words from Luana. The *not seeing* Luana, who had been avoiding him since the episode with Grantham. He'd decided to give her a few hours to cool off, but he'd been unable to connect with her since. Four and a half days!

And all along it was Stacey's boyfriend.

"So no one knows about the resort."

"As far as we know," Tommy said.

"Great. Just great." Jake was too upset to let it go. "And you couldn't call and tell me? No, you just let it drop casually. After I practically accused the resort people of being responsible. They weren't happy about it either, I can tell you. I challenged their sterling reputation for discretion and service, so you can't blame them. Especially now."

Callie's eyes widened, and she stared at the back of his head, all she could see from her position in the backseat.

"I'm going to take you to see the wedding coordinator first thing, Callie. And you're going to apologize to her for blaming her when you had no basis for it."

"Well, honestly, Jake."

"You wanted her fired, Callie." Jake heard his voice rising, but he couldn't help it. She should have called him immediately; it might have made all the difference. Not that it mattered about the hotel. They'd get over it. But Luana!

Callie leaned forward, ready to argue with her brother, but Tommy stopped her with a hand on her shoulder. He pulled her back, leaning close to whisper something in her ear.

Intent on driving, as well as controlling his anger, Jake barely noticed. When he saw their heads together in the rearview mirror, he thought they were going to start making out in the backseat, like the teenagers they were. Well, Tommy wasn't a teenager, technically, but sometimes he acted like one. Jake scowled, feeling every one of his own thirty years.

Callie's voice reached him a minute later, surprising him with a meek acceptance.

"Okay, Jake. I'd like to meet her, actually. I'm sure she's planned a beautiful wedding for us."

Jake wondered briefly what she was up to, but decided he didn't care, as long as Luana got her apology. He'd have to work up something to tell Grantham.

"I'll take you to see her as soon as we get there. It's going to be a beautiful wedding. I wouldn't want any hard feelings to spoil it."

Tommy leaned in and kissed Callie. Jake, caught between not understanding and wanting to be back in Luana's good graces, decided to get them there as quickly as possible. While Callie was in a good mood, and before she changed her mind.

Luana sat at her desk, finalizing arrangements for the Smith wedding. She was determined that it would be the best wedding the resort had ever seen. Nothing would interfere with this ceremony, if she had to capture and eliminate paparazzi on her own.

"Are you busy?"

The familiar words and voice made her heart lurch. How she'd looked forward to those words a few short days ago; before he'd had the audacity to blame her for leaking a story she didn't even know to the press. And not just any press, but those supermarket tabloids!

She had stayed away from the resort as much as possible over the past week, so she hadn't seen Jake. She'd heard from other employees that he'd asked for her several times but she hadn't let that sway her resolve. Trust was important between friends; it was essential between a couple.

Now she looked up, ready to tell him that she was indeed very busy, when a pert and sassy-looking blond stepped around him. She wore no makeup but sported tight jeans faded to a pale blue, and a loose-fitting T-shirt from the Hard Rock Café in London. She looked about twelve years old.

"I'm sure she has a minute for us," she said.

Her voice was smooth and confident. Trailing behind her, held by her hand, was a tall, thin, extremely good-looking young man. Undoubtedly, Luana was finally face to face with Callie and Mr. Smith.

Luana stood while Jake made the formal introductions, then offered her hand to the young couple. Luckily, Callie held Tommy with her left hand, because she didn't release him to shake hands with Luana. Tommy merely nodded, gesturing helplessly toward his incapacitated hand, an apologetic and boyish smile on his lips. Luana had to smile. Mele had been right about him. He was terribly cute and obviously smitten.

"How nice to finally meet you, Callie. Mr. Smith."

Luana smiled warmly, wanting to make the young couple feel welcome. Jake she tried to ignore.

"Call me Tommy."

"I know." Luana couldn't help but smile. "Mr. Smith is your dad."

"Yeah."

Luana liked the young man with his shy smile. No wonder young girls swooned over him. Mele would die if she was here, might even swoon herself.

But Callie was obviously the talker of the two.

"I wanted to stop by—*we* wanted to stop by—first thing to thank you for all the work you've done." Callie's voice was sincere. "I know it was hard for you with all the secrecy and everything. But you can see why it was necessary. And I want to apologize for ever blaming you and the resort for leaking word of the wedding." Her eyes sought Luana's as she continued in a sheepish voice. "Sometimes I jump to conclusions."

Callie's eyes were as blue as Jake's, Luana noticed, and they were looking right into her eyes, pleading for understanding.

When she heard Callie's next words, Luana wondered if the young woman was an actress as well as a singer. She could certainly put a lot of heartfelt emotion into her speech.

"It was all my fault, you know. I was so upset when I

saw that story about the wedding, I insisted that Jake do something, immediately." She grimaced, shrugging helplessly. "Jake told me it definitely was not you and the resort, but I wouldn't listen." She hung her head. "I've had problems before, you see. With people who get close and then sell out. It's kind of a professional hazard."

Luana's heart went out to the young woman who had apparently been betrayed by so-called friends.

Callie was continuing. "And then I discovered it was my maid of honor's sleazy boyfriend. What a jerk *he* turned out to be."

Beside her, Tommy nodded his agreement.

"So you'll forgive us, won't you?"

Callie smiled so sweetly at her, Luana could do little else. But she continued to avoid looking at Jake. *She* didn't jump to conclusions. She had first-hand information of Jake's betrayal.

But she would do her job. Callie and Tommy would have the loveliest wedding ever seen at the Kukui Wana'ao.

"Of course. I'm sure it's been a stressful time for you. Is there anything I can help you with?" She glanced from Callie to Tommy as she spoke. "The rehearsal will be this evening. I have some of the greenery in place in the ceremony room, but the flowers won't go in until tomorrow, of course. Jake said you like fragrant flowers, so I've ordered ginger and gardenia plants for the garden backdrop. There will be orchids, too, because they add so much atmosphere, but of course they don't have any scent to speak of."

"Sounds great." Callie turned dreamy eyes toward Tommy. "Doesn't it, Tommy?"

Tommy nodded.

"I'm sure everything will be perfect."

Once again, Tommy nodded his agreement.

Jake stepped forward, smiling warmly at Luana. "Callie and her party just arrived from the mainland. I'm sure you want to go to your room and rest for a bit, don't you, Callie?"

Callie looked from Luana to Jake and back again.

"Yeah. I do." She giggled at her words, reminiscent of the vows she would be exchanging the following evening. "We do, don't we, Tommy? Let's go. You can join us later, Jake. We'll be in Dad's room."

Callie turned back to Luana. "Thanks again, Luana. And I really am sorry about the mix-up."

Tommy still firmly attached to Callie's hand, the young couple left Luana's office.

Jake's voice was soft, as warm as a ray of sunshine. "I did tell her you couldn't have done it, you know. But I still had to ask you and the manager—as the only two people here who might know anything about the wedding."

Luana sat. Heavily. She suddenly felt very tired. She didn't want to go through this with Jake again. She should never have let herself get so close to him to begin with. The extreme pain she'd felt since his accusation was a wake-up call. She didn't plan to get back into that situation. She would do her job and keep her distance. So she made no comment to Jake's statement.

"Luana."

She glanced up, trying for a start of surprise. She failed, but then that was okay too. Jake would get the idea.

"Oh, are you still here, Mr. Lawrence?"

Jake groaned. "Please, Luana. I've been trying to reach you for the past four days. It's been killing me. You must have gotten my messages."

"I've been very busy. Was there something more I could help you with?"

Jake stared. What would she do if he gave her the truth? If he said, yes, you can love me. If he said, you can help me by marrying me, and spending the rest of your life with me.

But Luana retained her pleasant, impersonal expression, looking at his face but not quite meeting his eyes. She was either a world-class actress, or she just didn't care. He had to find some way to win her over. But he also had to get through the next two days and all the wedding activities. He didn't know what he was going to do about Luana. But he'd better think of something fast.

Chapter Thirteen

Luana found that the rehearsal wasn't as difficult as she had feared. Everything went as smoothly as could be expected for a rehearsal, and there were enough people involved that she easily avoided Jake. She was too busy to even worry about his presence.

In any case, he stayed beside his father when he wasn't in his place as best man. Reverend Johnston was a wonderful, hearty man, with a great sense of fun. He kept them all laughing, and Luana completely forgot that she was giving orders to some of the most popular singers in show business. Mele would die if she knew!

Luckily, Luana didn't have a spare moment to see Mele that day or the next. So there was no danger that she would be tempted to tell her about the resort guests, and no evading her friend's questions if she happened to hear anything of the resort's new celebrity arrivals.

The day of the wedding was picture perfect. Light, early-morning showers had cleared by the time the wedding party and guests began to appear for breakfast. Not that Luana expected any of the famous guests in the public dining areas. She'd noted the cautious way Callie, Tommy, and his fellow group members had entered the rehearsal room the night before. The downside of fame, she was told. Everything had to be carefully planned or you could cause a riot.

She hadn't believed Callie when she'd mentioned this to Luana, but Reverend Johnston had supported her. He claimed to have seen it happen when the boys went out for a snack in his own town.

"Right there where Monroe grew up, and they had to call out the cops and the fire department to get them safely home." He'd shaken his head, amazed at what success could bring.

Luana herself was up and running long before the time Jake used to arrive in her office with breakfast. She met the truck from the nursery and supervised the unloading and placement of the flowering plants. Then she had to situate all the cut-flower arrangements, and see to the reception-table centerpieces.

The rooms were fairly well set up by noon, and Luana was exhausted. She retreated to her office, hoping for a restful hour or two of quiet. She had brought along a change of clothes—still her official resort muumuu, but a fresh, clean one—for later.

As she checked and rechecked the arrangements for the evening's festivities, Luana was unable to keep Jake from her mind. He was too much a part of this wedding for her not to think of him at every turn.

The delivery of the framed artwork made from the paper cranes almost made her cry. How could she forget that wonderful day she had taught him to make them? What fun they'd had! She'd suspected him of being clumsy on purpose so that she would have to sit close and hold his hands to direct his fingers into making the proper folds. But she'd enjoyed that as much as he had.

And he'd brought her the wonderful photographs of her friends that day, too.

Luana took the heavy frame into the reception room and set it on an easel, already in place near the table which held the guest book. The initials C and T were artfully intertwined in the center of a large golden circle on a black background. A few leaves in each corner set the whole off perfectly. Luana stared at the letters, wondering if J and L would have made such a beautiful design. Then she shook her head in disgust and turned to leave. And walked straight into Jake's chest.

"Everything is looking terrific, Luana." His eyes scanned the room before settling on the frame she had just set down. "Callie will be thrilled with your cranes."

"They aren't mine—"

But Jake interrupted. "You know what I mean. We wouldn't have known anything about it if you hadn't told me of the custom. And guided me through the making of the cranes so I could teach her."

Slowly, his glance moved back to Luana, then returned to the frame. "I wonder how J and L would look, intertwined. . . ."

Luana turned and fled before he could finish his thought. He'd always seemed to know what she was thinking. It was positively uncanny. Especially now that they were estranged, and likely to remain that way. Trust was so important between two people trying to forge a relationship and he had shown that there was none between them. It broke her heart to leave when he was attempting a reconciliation, but how could she stay, knowing he hadn't trusted her?

Her heart was pounding by the time she arrived at her office and closed the door firmly behind her. She had to get away from Jake. She had the whole evening still to get through before she could be done with him. And she didn't know how she would manage.

Luana sank down into her chair. She propped her elbows on the desk in front of her and dropped her head onto her palms. As she tried to hide from the pain of being near Jake, something Emma said to her returned. What was it? Something about almost missing what was right there in front of her. That was it. *"Don't let some disagreement get in the way of your happiness. I almost lost Matt because I was too blind to see what I had."* And then she'd added, *"Love is the most important thing of all."*

Luana's head flew up. How on earth had she remembered all that? It must be because it was important. She'd always wondered about people who claimed a guardian angel had stepped in to save them from whatever problem they faced. Could this be *her* guardian angel, finally stepping in? Helping her remember Emma's advice? She'd never not believed in angels, merely wondered if they would involve themselves in such petty human concerns.

Petty concerns. Was she letting a petty disagreement come between her and happiness? If that was true, then it wasn't such a petty concern, was it?

Luana reflected on Jake, on the happiness she felt when they were together. They enjoyed the same things, laughed over the same things. Both of them liked to argue a point from both sides.

"I wonder how J and L would look, intertwined. . . ."

Luana had heard his words, the same words she herself had thought just moments before. And this phenomenon had happened time and again throughout their acquaintance.

Luana's thoughts moved to Jake, a professional man, an admitted workaholic, who had abandoned his beloved career for a month to take on the unfamiliar task of putting on a wedding—as a favor to his young half-sister. There had to be a lot of good in a man who would consent to do that.

She remembered his excellent manners, his sincere interest in Hawaiian music and culture.

Luana groaned. She was going to lose a remarkable man, the man she loved, because she had refused to accept his sincere apology. How foolish she'd been. Because now she knew Emma to be correct. Love was the most important thing of all. And she did love Jake.

Was it too late?

Unfortunately, Luana thought it might be. She didn't see Jake again until just before the ceremony, when he passed through the rooms with the security detail. She couldn't very well approach him to admit her love when he was with the resort security people.

The next thing she knew, the guests were being escorted into the room, and she was showing Reverend Johnston, Jake, and the men of Four-by-Six into a small anteroom where they could wait until it was time for them to appear. Callie, her father, and her attendants were safely ensconced in a larger room nearby.

Luana found herself being pulled in four different directions as she worked out last-minute problems, many of them merely caused by nerves.

Hours later, Luana was ready to breathe a sigh of relief. The wedding had gone splendidly, the bride and groom had made it safely from one room to another without attracting any undue attention, and the security force reported no signs of photographers or reporters sneaking onto the grounds. Guests had raved about her beautiful garden in the ceremony room, and admired the decor in the reception room. Dinner had been served, and one of the guests serving as disc jockey had begun the dancing.

Luana stood in what she hoped was an unobtrusive corner, observing the activity in the room and wondering if she could safely sneak away, when Callie came dashing over.

"Luana, I'm so glad you're still here."

So much for sneaking off, Luana thought. She'd better stick around all night, just in case. Mr. Grantham was sure to think Callie an even more important guest than Jake. And tonight *was* her last chance to catch Jake alone.

So she disregarded her tired feet and summoned a cheerful smile for the new bride.

"What is it, Callie?"

"The DJ wants to do some kind of little game later, and he'll need about six chairs. Do you have any more, so we don't have to take them from the tables?"

"Certainly. I'll get them right away."

"Great. Thanks."

Luana spoke to one of the waiters, telling him that she would need more chairs, asking him to meet her at the storage room down the hall to help carry them back. Then she headed there herself.

Normally, the storage areas would be kept open during

a party, for the convenience of the staff. But because of the heightened security for this event, all the doors in the immediate area were locked. Luana would have to unlock the door before anyone could remove the chairs.

She unlocked the door, propped it open, then stepped inside to locate the chairs they would need. She hated these narrow storage rooms, but at least with the door open it didn't seem so stifling.

Folding chairs would probably work, Luana decided, and they would be easy to carry. They were also the closest to the door. She was removing six of them from the stack on one of the wheeled platforms when she heard a step behind her.

"Just in time. I'll have them in just a second."

Luana turned, thinking to see the waiter she'd just spoken to. Instead, Jake Lawrence stood behind her. The chairs in her hands clattered to the floor, barely missing her toes.

"What are you doing here?"

Before he could answer, there was a swoosh of air and the door closed with a loud, decisive click. Luana had a terrible feeling that they had just been locked in. Locked into a small storage closet with Jake Lawrence!

Luana flew past Jake to the door and her hand closed over the handle. It wasn't a round knob, but one of the straight types that moved downward to open the door. Which shouldn't be locked. Wasn't there a fire code requiring that doors be able to open from the inside?

The room seemed smaller than ever, and there were no windows, of course. Not in a room that was little more than a storage locker. Forgetting that she was now alone with Jake, a happening she had been hoping for all afternoon, Luana stood before the door and grasped the handle. Panicking, she pushed at the metal, shaking the door in its frame but doing little else.

"Luana."

Jake's voice was gentle, and came from just over her right shoulder. His hand settled lightly on her shoulder.

"Luana, do you suffer from claustrophobia?"

Luana turned, shocked at how close he was in the confined space. She shouldn't have been. She'd been feeling the heat of his body from the moment he stepped into the small room.

"Why? Did you plan this, and only now you're thinking of the consequences?" She was frightened and near tears. Her hope to reconcile with Jake was far from her mind.

"I didn't plan this. I know nothing about it. Callie told me you needed some help bringing in a few extra chairs."

His voice was sincere, his expression earnest. Luana tried hard to listen, but the walls seemed to be closing in on her. She couldn't concentrate.

His voice remained gentle. "It's Callie. She thinks she's helping us."

Despite herself, Luana felt tears gathering. She didn't like small, confined spaces. At least it wasn't dark, but what if the light went off? How reliable were the lights in here?

She forced her thoughts away from her predicament, taking a deep breath and trying to concentrate on Jake's words. Callie.

"What is it she thinks she's helping?"

"Callie has an artist's temperament. She blows up over things—sometimes little things. Then the next time she sees you, she's all sweetness and apologies. When she saw news of the wedding in the tabloid, she didn't want to blame any of her close friends, so she figured it had to be the resort. Or you."

Luana's frowned. "I don't see—"

"You're not listening." Jake's voice remained quiet, cast

low and intimate. "Just before she arrived here she discovered it was Stacey's boyfriend who sold them the news. You met Stacey, she's the maid of honor."

Luana nodded. Reluctantly. Concentrating on his words, looking into his eyes, seemed to help keep her mind off the situation.

His wry smile made Luana's knees weak.

"Callie realized how unhappy I was about how her assumptions affected you and ruined our friendship. So she must have decided she had to do something to help."

"You were unhappy?" Luana's eyes searched his face.

Jake nodded solemnly.

"I was very unhappy. I told her she had accused you and the resort, and she'd better apologize to you personally. I was mad. It was because she was so sure that the leak came from here that I brought it up that day. And I couldn't confront Grantham without bringing you into it. And you were deeply offended, as you had every right to be."

Luana didn't know when she'd moved, or even if she had. But suddenly, they were standing toe to toe. One tiny movement on either person's part and they would be in each other's arms.

"I've missed you, Luana." Jake raised his hand, brushing his fingers lightly down her cheek. "We haven't known each other long, but I knew from the start that you were the one for me."

Luana closed her eyes as his touch shivered through her. When she opened them again, he was even closer if possible, his eyes intense as they stared into hers. His nearness was so much less frightening than the closeness of the small room's walls. When he placed his hands lightly on her upper arms, she wanted to dissolve against him. She felt sure that being in his arms would bring the ultimate comfort to her spirit.

Luana was so distracted by his presence, she almost missed what he was saying. But something about the intensity of his voice seeped into her consciousness, and she found herself listening with rapt attention.

"I know you're a very organized person, Luana, that you like everything planned out in advance. That's why you're so good at organizing weddings. But do something impetuous for once. Marry me."

His head was *very* close now, his hands running lightly up and down her upper arms. His eyes were huge, her reflection staring back at her from them. Luana felt oddly detached as she examined herself, using his eyes as a mirror. She looked surprised, her eyes almost as large as his, her lips slightly parted.

Then she saw her mouth soften, begin to part in a smile. What difference did it make if he lived in California? Planes traveled the distance every day. Phones could keep one in constant contact with family and friends.

Her smile widened. Wasn't love the most important thing of all? They would create their own home, their own family.

And then Jake closed that last small distance, so that she could no longer see herself. Or his eyes. His lips touched hers, tentatively, then retreated. Luana felt lost. She wanted his lips back on hers.

"You haven't answered my question, Luana."

Almost a whisper. She could feel the breath caused by his words brushing over her lips.

"Was it a question?"

Her voice was no louder than his. Her arms snaked

around to his back and she pressed into him. She wanted him to hold her, and she wanted his kiss.

"Will you marry me?"

"Yes."

His lips settled over hers, his arms enclosing her tightly against him. He felt so good. He was warm and gentle, firm and possessive, protecting and strong.

The cool breeze of the air-conditioning flooded over them, the dimness of the room's lighting suddenly brightening as it was augmented by the lobby lights.

"Jake! Hey, big brother. Is it over? I don't want to miss all the dancing."

Callie strutted into the room, closely followed by Tommy. "Have you got an announcement to make?"

Luana was embarrassed, stepping quickly away from Jake. No wonder the door wouldn't open. They must have been holding tight to the door handle, or found something to jam under it.

Jake, however, wouldn't let Luana stray too far from his side, pulling her tight against him. He grinned at his sister and her new husband, even as he scolded them.

"Callie Lawrence, you have some explaining to do!"

"Aw, come on, Jake. Besides, it's Callie Smith now," she added with a teasing grin. "And about that announcement . . . ?"

Jake pulled Luana even closer, his arm firm across her shoulders. "You may be the first to congratulate us. Luana has consented to be my wife."

"*Ya-hoo!*"

Luana's eyes widened in shock at the wild shout, which bounced off the walls of the small room. She suddenly remembered Mele telling her that Callie had started out as a country-western singer.

Callie flew forward, throwing her arms around both Jake and Luana. "I'm so excited. Another wedding! What fun!"

Callie reached for Tommy's hand and headed for the door. "Don't worry about the chairs," she called over her shoulder. "We won't be needing them after all."

Jake and Luana exchanged a look. So Jake had been right. The whole chair episode had been engineered by Callie to bring them back together.

Callie pivoted on the ball of her foot and started back down the hall to the reception room. She stopped a few feet away, gesturing impatiently for them to follow.

"Come on. It's almost time to toss the bouquet. And I want to see Luana right in front," she said. She flashed a big smile, adding a saucy wink at Luana.

Jake followed the new Mr. and Mrs. Smith, pulling Luana along with his arm around her waist. Luana was reluctant to join the party. She had no business being there as one of the guests; she was still employed by the hotel.

But Jake refused to recognize her embarrassment.

"Jake," she whispered urgently. "I can't join Callie's friends."

"Why not?"

"Look at them." Luana let her exasperation taint her voice. "Look at their clothes. Look at me." Surely a man as sophisticated as Jake could see that the cost of just one of the outfits in that room could supply her with clothes for a year.

But Jake laughed.

"You look terrific."

They were still disagreeing when they arrived at the reception hall. Callie's voice rang out over the crowd.

"Time to throw the bouquet."

The single women in the room immediately gathered on

the dance floor, their noisy chatter filling the large room. There were a lot of them, Luana noticed. She tried to shrink back against the wall. Callie wouldn't even know she wasn't there.

Jake remained at her side. Now he grinned down at her. "She won't throw it until you go over there, you know."

"How will she know I'm not there? There must be forty women out there."

Jake smiled fondly. "Once Callie decides on something, she always manages to get her way. And I think she's decided you're going to catch her bouquet."

"But—"

Luana didn't have an opportunity to express an opinion of her own. From across the room, Callie's voice carried over to her.

"Luana Young, you get over here."

Luana felt the heat all the way from her forehead to her throat. She wanted the floor to open up and swallow her. But Jake, the scoundrel, led her onto the floor himself. She saw the curious looks the others gave her, heard the whispers behind her. But mostly, she saw Callie's determined face, heard Jake's voice saying "she always manages to get her way." She'd gotten him to take a vacation, hadn't she? She'd gotten her wonderful, secret wedding.

Luana took her place amid the crowd of young women.

Callie scanned the group with her eyes, a mischievous smile playing at her lips. Then she turned and flipped the small throwing bouquet over her head.

Luana stood in place, determined not to make any attempt to catch the bouquet. It wasn't her place. She was the wedding coordinator.

She'd planned without taking into consideration Callie's determination and her unerring aim. The bouquet sailed high over the young bride's head, and floated across the six feet or so of dance floor behind her—to land smack against Luana's blue-and-purple chest. Without thought, she brought her hands up to clutch the flowers.

Luana heard some moans of disappointment behind her, but Callie turned, and let out a loud rebel yell.

"Ladies and gentlemen."

For such a tiny woman, Luana thought, Callie had a voice that could carry across a football field. Then she remembered what the petite woman did for a living and realized that, of course she did.

As though he knew what was to come, Jake approached Luana and put his hand around her waist. He pulled her close, and dropped a kiss on her forehead.

"Jake, I can't take this." Luana gestured to the flowers she held.

But Jake shushed her. "Listen to Callie."

"I have an announcement to make."

Callie's commanding voice brought the room to a hush. She tossed an impish smile toward first Jake, then their father.

"See that pretty lady who caught my bouquet?"

Luana saw every face in the room turn in her direction. She didn't know how red her face might be, but by now it felt hot enough to be the color of tomato soup.

"That's Luana Young, who arranged this wonderful wedding for Tommy and me." Callie paused, to lead the group in a round of applause for Luana.

"However, tonight, I have a big announcement to make. A huge one, in fact. I want to announce the engagement of my brother, Jake, to Luana."

Callie led the room in raucous applause. Jake took advantage of the moment to gather Luana into his arms for a kiss. The applause went up a notch, some of the onlookers adding shouts of encouragement. Jake and Luana barely noticed. They could have been alone in the room as they stood together, holding on to each other, their lips tasting and exploring.

Finally, Jake pulled back. He turned Luana into the room, and bowed slightly to acknowledge the good wishes of the crowd. Then he turned and fled, pulling Luana along with him. He didn't even hear Callie shouting after him about Tommy tossing the garter.

Laughing, the escaping duo stopped down the hall, outside the door to the infamous storage room.

"Now that Callie has announced to the world that we're getting married, we'll have to go tell my parents."

"We'll leave in a minute." Jake's head lowered and his breath feathered across her forehead. "More important, *when* shall we get married?" His smile danced across his mouth, and Luana knew he wanted to kiss her again. "Are you going to make me wait a whole year while you plan something spectacular?"

"Maybe." Luana teased with her eyes.

Jake groaned. "Haven't you been planning your own wedding forever? Tell me you don't need a whole year."

Luana was so tickled that he was willing to wait a year, she hadn't the heart to require it.

"I know a lot about weddings now," Jake told her. "I even know how to help with the origami cranes." He dropped a kiss at the corner of her eye.

"Six months?"

Jake groaned again, but he nodded.

Luana moved her head, hoping to catch his mouth for another kiss. She had six months to plan the most wonderful wedding the island had ever seen. She deserved it. And she knew Jake would agree.